THE RUTHLESS MEN

THE RUTHLESS MEN

LEWIS B. PATTEN

THORNDIKE
CHIVERS

LIBRARY OF CONGRESS CATALOGING-IN-PUBLICATION DATA

Patten, Lewis B.
  The ruthless men / by Lewis B. Patten.
    p. cm. — (Thorndike Press large print Western)
    ISBN-13: 978-1-4104-2448-8 (alk. paper)
    ISBN-10: 1-4104-2448-0 (alk. paper)
    1. Large type books. I. Title.
PS3566.A79R78 2010
813'.54—dc22   2009049094

BRITISH LIBRARY CATALOGUING-IN-PUBLICATION DATA AVAILABLE

Published in 2010 in the U.S. by arrangement with Golden West Literary Agency.
Published in 2010 in the U.K. by arrangement with Golden West Literary Agency.

U.K. Hardcover: 978 1 408 49092 1 (Chivers Large Print)
U.K. Softcover: 978 1 408 49093 8 (Camden Large Print)

THE RUTHLESS MEN

CHAPTER ONE

Luke Partin pulled his sweating, plodding horse to a halt on top of the rise and stared at the town below.

He was dusty and beat, but the bleakness had not faded from his eyes. Nor had the hot, implacable anger that smouldered there.

He'd been gaining for two days, and the trail he followed was now very, very fresh.

He'd accomplished it mostly by guessing — and guessing right. Still, there weren't too many towns here in central Texas, and almost from the first it had been apparent that his quarry was heading straight for this one.

Luke had never told himself that this was none of his affair, that it was a thing for the law to settle. Law was scarce in this land, and too often a man must make his own. Besides, this was an animal he pursued —

not a man. No man, no human thing could do the things to the Ortiz family that this one had.

Still strongly etched in Luke's mind was the sight that had greeted him at the Ortiz place. The ransacked and ruined house. Miguel Ortiz, tied to a chair, staring with sightless eyes at the naked, mutilated body of his daughter, Juana, who was barely in her teens. And Mrs. Ortiz, her skull smashed, lying a few short feet away . . .

For what? It was hard to decide. Luke had known them many years and was certain there couldn't have been more than a few pesos in that squalid adobe shack.

But there had been other things — kindness, compassion, human wisdom and tolerance. Luke was alive because of the Ortiz family. Wounded by Apaches and near death, he had once crawled on his stomach to that shack.

Memory made his jaw harden. An animal had done it — an animal who hurt for the sake of hurting, who killed when he could hurt no more, who then tore apart a room with a kind of bestial frenzy looking for a pitiful hoard of cash.

Trailing him, Luke had seen the man but once — close enough to fire at him twice. Close enough to know him by his big, hulking frame, by his dress and by the horse he rode.

He'd lost him after that when night and darkness came. But the following morning he had picked up his trail again.

Always it led north, as though the fugitive had in his twisted mind a specific destination where safety lay.

Luke talked with those he met along his way. Towns were scarce ahead. But one lay directly along the fugitive's route.

After he discovered that, Luke began to travel at night himself. He began to gain steadily, though he intermittently lost the trail.

Casting back and forth each morning he had always found it again. And now he was here, surely at the end of the long, long trail.

Luke was a tall, lean man. Excess bulk had long since been sweated and worked off his lanky frame, but there was an ease and quickness about his movements that bespoke surprising strength.

His face was as lean as his frame, burned dark by the desert sun, with hollow cheeks and high, pointed cheekbones that made him look as though he might well have some Indian ancestry.

His eyes were dark, seeming at times almost black. They could be soft, though they seldom were. Certainly they weren't soft now. They were like bits of black stone set in the dark mahogany of his face.

His hair, that which showed beneath his dusty, wide-brimmed hat, was beginning to grey though he was only thirty-two. This land did that to a man — this land and the hard, unending struggle just to stay alive.

The main street of Comanche Wells was shaded by gigantic cottonwoods. Their branches spread across it until they met and entwined in the middle. Dogs slept in the shady dust. A couple of red chickens scratched under the feed store dock.

Tension came to Luke Partin now. His man was here. The trail he followed leading down towards town was less than half an hour old.

Coldly angry, he entered the street and let his horse pick an aimless way along its dusty length. His eyes roved back and forth ceaselessly. The man knew Luke was on his trail, though he probably didn't know how close.

The town was built largely of adobe bricks, plastered with reddish mud. The only frame buildings were the church, two false-fronted stores, a garishly ornate hotel, and a couple of houses a block off Main.

There was a saloon of adobe with a small

courtyard holding a well and pump. A restaurant next door emitted odours of spicy Mexican food.

Luke didn't notice the restaurant. He didn't smell the food. He had eyes for but one thing — a dusty bay horse standing at the rail outside the courtyard of the saloon.

He knew that horse. He should. He had followed it several hundred miles.

He dismounted and tied his horse beside the bay. He touched the grips of the Confederate Dance Brothers and Park revolver, loosening it in its holster at his side.

His anger was cold, now that the time was here. The man would have his chance. But he would die.

Luke crossed the shady courtyard, not feeling the delicious coolness of the shade. His body was tense, his eyes narrowed, never leaving the door of the saloon except to flick once or twice to the narrow window.

Voices droned inside the saloon, floating out through the open doors. Luke stepped on through.

He moved aside almost instantly and stood against one tied-back door. There were five men in the saloon, of which the bartender was one. Only one of the others was large enough to be the one Luke sought.

Big he was, full-bearded and ponderous.

A man with a narrow, sloping forehead and piggish, close-set eyes.

His clothes were dusty and stained with sweat. Already he had finished a third of the bottle before him, and his eyes showed it.

He looked at Luke and froze. Luke said savagely, coldly, "You know why I'm here. I'm going to kill you, right where you stand. It's a better chance than you gave Miguel Ortiz and his family, but I'm going to let you go for that gun you've got."

He could see the feigned surprise coming into the big man's eyes. He could see how hard the man tried to look puzzled.

The man's voice was rough, raspy, both from dryness and the whisky he had consumed. "I don't know what the hell you're talkin' about. Get out of here and let me be."

"You're a liar. You're not only a liar, but you're a stinking butcher too. I'll count to three. When I finish the count, you'd better grab your gun because I'll be grabbing mine."

His eyes flicked to the bartender — to the other three standing at the bar. "A private quarrel. Going to leave it that way?"

The bartender nodded, his face white, his mouth twitching. The others followed suit.

Luke said, "One."

The big man shifted. Panic touched his eyes. He switched his glance to the bartender, to the three a few feet away along the bar. He said, "Somebody better stop this. Or they'll wish they had."

Luke said, "Two."

The big man's shoulder twitched, but then he changed his mind.

Luke said, "Three."

He waited an instant, every muscle in his body tense. The big man didn't move.

Luke willed his hand to grab his gun, but it stayed frozen at his side, inches away from the grips.

Angrily he thought of the Ortiz family, making his mind remember each bloody detail. Still he couldn't move his hand. He could kill this man but he couldn't execute him. No matter how he tried.

He stepped into the doorway deliberately. "Looks like you need better odds." He turned his back recklessly and took a step out through the door.

He heard the movement behind him. He heard it and a fierce exultation leaped in his mind. Now his hand shot to his side and closed around the grips of his gun.

He started to turn, gun clearing the holster and raising as the hammer came back.

Behind him, inside the saloon, a gun blasted. Something seared along Luke's ribs, burning like an iron. Almost instantly his side was drenched with blood.

He continued his turn, knowing the second shot was coming, knowing the first would have killed him but for the warning of that soft whisper of sound.

Instinct raised his gun; instinct centred it and tightened the tendons of his forefinger.

The bullet struck the big man squarely between the eyes at the precise instant he squeezed off his second shot.

This one tore through the muscles of Luke's left arm.

He holstered his gun and stepped inside, feeling blood running down his arm. He looked at the white-faced three, at the bartender rounding the bar at a run. He said, "He hit me twice. Will somebody get the law so I can get this settled up?"

It was done now, done. But his anger hadn't left. Nor was he satisfied. He looked down at the ponderous hulk of dead flesh at his feet, hating the man still, hating him even in death the way you hate a dead rattlesnake, no less repulsive in death than it is in life.

The bartender sent one of the men for the sheriff, then hustled to Luke's side. "Hit bad, mister?"

Luke shook his head. "I've been hit worse."

"Come over here and sit down. I'll tie them places up and give you a couple of drinks to ease the pain." He shook his head. "God, that was quick!"

Yes. It *had* been quick. Too quick. Too soon over to ease the outrage and fury that had smouldered these many days in Luke Partin's heart.

Luke followed the bartender and sat down. He stripped off his shirt, wincing at the pain. The bartender poured whisky into a clean towel and mopped at the bloody wounds, first the one in Luke's side, after that the one in his arm.

Luke moved the hurt arm tentatively. His face twisted as he did, but relief showed in his eyes. The muscle might be torn but it wasn't torn badly enough to spoil his use of the arm.

The bartender now ripped a clean bar towel into strips and began to bandage the bullet burn on his ribs. Luke felt light-headed and hung his head between his knees, a kind of desperation touching him. If he passed out now . . .

The weakness passed. He looked up in time to see a blocky, oldish man with a star pinned to his shirt come through the door.

The man said irritably, "What's happened now, Jake?" He saw the body and breathed, "Oh Hell! Spence Maxfield!"

The bartender said, "This stranger came bustin' in tellin' Spence to draw. Said he was goin' to kill him. Spence wouldn't fight, so the stranger turned his back and started out. Spence shot him then. Twice. Stranger stayed on his feet and put one right between Spence's eyes."

The sheriff looked tired and a little scared. He stared at Luke appraisingly, finally asking, "What'd you want him for?"

"Killing three of my friends. A man, a woman, and a girl no more'n fourteen."

The sheriff didn't comment. It was apparent to Luke that he didn't doubt the charge. He said to Luke, "How bad are you hurt?"

"Bullet burn on the ribs. Another one on my arm."

"Can you travel?"

"Don't know why not." Luke thought he detected something strange in the look of both the sheriff and the bartender. He glanced up at the sheriff. "Then I'm free to go?"

"You sure are. In fact, I'd advise it. Spence has got seven brothers and an old man just as mean as he was. They ain't goin' to like your pluggin' him."

Luke shrugged. "I suppose not." He didn't give a damn about Spence Maxfield's brothers or his father either. But he would like to tell them what their precious Spence had done.

The bartender finished bandaging his arm. He put on his shirt which was sodden with blood and felt both cold and sticky against his skin. He got up, swayed, shook his head angrily and stepped to the bar. Jake went around behind it and shoved a bottle and a glass across to him. "On the house."

Luke poured a stiff one and drank it. He pushed the bottle away. One of the three who had been in the saloon was whispering to the sheriff. The sheriff left him and approached Luke, his face grave. "Dan says somebody's already gone for the Maxfield clan. Spence must've known you were after him. He sent Fitch Gowan out soon's he hit town."

Luke scowled. This explained Spence's hurry to get to Comanche Wells. He'd known his brothers and father would back him up. But he'd thought Luke was far enough behind so that he could afford a few drinks while someone else went after the clan. Only he'd been wrong.

The sheriff asked, "Need a fresh horse?

John Wilse's stable is the best place in town to trade . . .

Obscure irritation touched Luke. "They've sure as hell got you buffaloed, haven't they?"

The sheriff's face darkened. He glared at Luke. "There's eight men out at the Maxfield place, only sixteen miles northeast of town, and every one of 'em is just as bad as Spence. You don't fight one Maxfield — you fight 'em all, because that's the way they are. When they find out you've killed Spence, they won't care why. They'll drop whatever they're doin' and stay with you until you're dead."

He paused. It was hot in the saloon and the sheriff's shirt was wet on chest and back and under the arms with sweat. He said wearily, "Don't get the idea I'm goin' to fight for you. All I got is your word that Spence done what you say he did. Don't think the town will fight 'em for you either. You don't mean a thing to us. So if you want to stay alive, get a horse and ride."

Luke's jaw hardened stubbornly. He stepped around the sheriff. "I'm going to eat."

Luke had run often enough, God knew. From Indians. From the Rurales. Once or twice from a posse. But he'd never liked it and he didn't like it now. He never would.

Nor had his outraged anger faded enough for him to run. Killing Spence hadn't paid for the deaths of the Ortiz family. He'd thought it would, but it hadn't. Maybe telling Spence Maxfield's father what kind of butcher he had spawned would finally kill his smouldering rage.

White-faced and angry, he pushed out of the saloon and headed for the restaurant next door.

Chapter Two

Luke stepped into the restaurant and took a stool at the counter. He was beginning to feel sick, and his nausea wasn't helped by the strong, spicy odour of cooking food.

A young, pretty Mexican girl in a limp apron came to take his order. He said, "Coffee. When I've finished that maybe I'll have something else."

He drank the coffee, forcing it into his rebellious stomach. Sixteen miles, the sheriff had said. Even if Fitch Gowan crowded his horse all the way, in this heat it would take him a couple of hours to get there. Add a couple more that it would take the Maxfields to get to town.

An hour had already passed since Gowan left. So Luke had three before the clan arrived. Three at least.

He'd been hungry when he rode into town, but he wasn't hungry now. The two wounds had spoiled his appetite.

Or maybe it was something else — maybe it was the sudden letdown of his pent-up anger. Maybe it was nausea born of staring down at Spence Maxfield's dead body. He'd felt very much the way a man feels staring at the coils of a rattlesnake he has killed.

He paid for the coffee and got to his feet. He went out, untied his horse from the rail before the saloon and rode to John Wilse's livery barn, a huge, adobe building with an odorous corral behind it.

Leaving there, he walked to the hotel and took a room. He climbed the stairs, suddenly exhausted, went into the room and closed the door behind him.

He lay down, fully clothed, on the bed, placing his gun beside him. He'd go back now, he supposed. He'd go back to branding cattle in the brush country west of the Colorado. There was no market for them, but there would be some day. He went to sleep, or slipped into unconsciousness, with that last thought.

The sheriff woke him at four o'clock. The room he had taken was on the second storey of the hotel and Luke had forgotten to draw the shades.

It was like an oven. His whole body was bathed with sweat. Blood had soaked through both bandages, through his shirt, and had spotted the sheet on which he lay.

The sheriff was shaking his unhurt shoulder frantically. "Wake up, man! Wake up!"

Luke started violently and sat up. His precaution of placing his gun beside him had been useless. The Maxfields could have entered the room as easily as the sheriff had.

The sheriff said urgently, "They're here, an' they're lookin' for you. Damn it, if you'd gotten out when I told you to, you'd have a three-hour start. Now . . ."

Luke stood up and winced. His side had stiffened until it was something of a chore just to stand straight. And there wasn't a single position in which he could hold his arm so that it didn't throb.

More important than that, his anger was gone, drained out of him like the blood he had lost. It didn't seem very important now that he face the Maxfields. He could see that doing so would only result in more killing, and there had already been enough of that.

If he could slip out now, without being seen, he could put enough distance between himself and Commanche Wells so that they probably wouldn't even follow.

The sheriff was saying, "Don't go back south. Too many towns and ranches that way to make it easy for them to trail. Ride north, into Comanche country. Believe me, Comanches are easy to face compared to that Maxfield bunch."

Luke nodded. It didn't really matter which direction he rode. All he wanted to do now was forget.

He said, "I've got to settle up for the room."

"Forget that," snapped the sheriff. "I'll take care of it. Just get going. Your horse is out in back."

Luke nodded. He sat down on the edge of the bed and pulled on his boots. He got up and took a long, tepid drink from the pitcher on the bureau. He started after the sheriff.

Angry voices down in the street made him pause. And other sounds. He crossed the room and pulled aside the yellowed curtain.

His room faced across the street towards the saloon in which he had killed Spence Maxfield. There were half a dozen men in the courtyard now, and their horses were grouped in front, a seventh holding them.

Two of the men were holding erect the sagging, nearly unconscious body of the bartender who had bound up Partin's wounds. Another was systematically pounding his bleeding face with his fists.

The bartender offered no resistance. But

he was stubbornly refusing to answer their angrily shouted question, "Which way did he go? You son-of-a-bitch, which way?"

The sheriff tugged at Partin's sleeve. "Come on, man, come on! Jake won't tell 'em anything!"

Luke stared at him briefly, incredulously. Then he poked his revolver muzzle out the window.

He laid a bullet in the dust at the feet of the man who was beating Jake. The man's head swung around, his eyes searching. Luke yelled, "Here! Over here, you bastard!"

He ducked back. The sheriff ran for the door, with Luke crowding him from behind. Bullets sprayed the window, shattering the glass, thudding into the walls. One went through the door panel a few inches above Luke's head.

The sheriff went down the back stairs, running. He panted exasperatedly, "You damn stupid fool! Now you ain't got a chance to get away."

"What was I supposed to do — let 'em beat Jake half to death?"

"He could of talked if he'd wanted to."

Luke stared at his back in disgust.

Sleep had refreshed him, and he was hungry now. But there wasn't time for that. He noticed a sack tied behind his saddle and looked at the sheriff inquiringly.

"Grub. Eat it on the trail. Now move, damn it!"

Luke swung stiffly to the saddle. He spurred away towards the alley's end.

His horse had gone less than half a dozen lengths before he saw two men swing, galloping, into the alley. Big men on big horses. One of them bawled, "There's the bastard!"

Luke whirled his horse, rearing. He set his spurs. The sheriff had a gun in his hand but it didn't look as though he meant to use it.

Luke thundered past him, leaning low. Eight men, and they ruled this town.

A couple of shots racketed down the alley. A third. A fourth. The bullets ricocheted against the hard-packed ground, against the adobe walls on either side.

He'd lived through many things, many chases and many fights. He wondered if he would die, now, in this dirty alley at the hands of the Maxfields.

He saw an opening between two adobe shacks. He reined over and, as he did, looked around.

The sheriff was down, oddly crumpled and very still. The two Maxfields thundered past his body.

Luke's horse sailed over a low, sagging picket fence, pounded through a litter of cans and broken boards, and burst out into a scattering of shacks on the outer edge of town.

Luke hesitated but a fraction of a second over his choice. Then he swung north with a tiny shrug. Looking back, he saw those two, and three others, converging on him.

He eased his rifle out of the boot. He had to slow them down. He had to have *some* start.

He levered a shell into the chamber and aimed carefully at one of the two who had followed him down the alley. He fired.

His bullet struck low, squarely in the middle of the horse's chest. The animal went down and his rider sailed over his head, rolling a dozen yards.

Luke was in the open now, on the flat, wide land, reining his horse back and forth to avoid their bullets. Glancing back, he saw that the four remaining riders had converged on the downed one. Two had dismounted and were shooting at him with rifles. The other two seemed to be talking to the fifth, who had picked himself up from the ground and was limping towards his dead horse.

As Luke watched, three more horsemen rode out from the town and approached the group.

Eight. Eight Maxfields, each as mean, according to the sheriff, as the dead Spence Maxfield had been. But he'd slowed them down and could now get out in front by a mile at least before they replaced the dead horse and came on again. A mile might be enough to last until dark.

A disquieting thought troubled him. The sheriff was dead. No one save Luke and the two Maxfields had been in the alley with him at the time of his death.

It didn't take much perception to tell who was going to be accused of the killing. The townspeople might know better, but as cowed as they were, they probably wouldn't dare speak up.

So now the Maxfields had a double reason for wanting Luke. To avenge Spence and to set up a goat for the sheriff's murder. He knew that if they caught him, he'd be dead when they brought him back to town.

And even if he managed to get away, they'd fix it so that he'd be a wanted outlaw with a price on his head.

Alf Maxfield picked himself up from the ground, half stunned, and limped back towards his dead horse. His brothers, Will, Gabe and Ezra, wheeled towards him when they saw he was down. His other brother, Vic, with whom he had been riding, turned reluctantly and came back. Will and Vic dismounted and began to fire at the fleeing stranger with their rifles.

Alf was the youngest of the clan, dirty and unshaven, yet not possessing what could be called a beard. It was more an untidy, yellow fuzz, beneath which his face was covered with angry-looking boils.

A stream of curses bubbled from his lips. He yanked his rifle from beneath his dead horse, flopped behind it and rested the rifle on the horse's belly. He began to fire methodically and with vicious concentration.

Gabe, the oldest, watched, his face expressionless. He turned his head briefly to say, "Too far for good shootin'. Ezra, ride back to town and get a horse for Alf."

Ezra rode away. Three others were approaching now from town; these were Miles, the old man, and Mart and Les.

Alf gave up. Gabe stared at him speculatively. "You kill the sheriff?"

Alf nodded, his face sheepish like that of a boy caught in some minor mischief.

"Anybody see you?"

"Nobody was in the alley but the sheriff, that stranger, an' me an' Vic."

"Sure?"

"I said so, didn't I?"

Gabe studied him a moment more. "All

right. Then all we got to do is bring that stranger back."

Gabe was almost forty, and while Miles was the nominal head of the family, Gabe was its real head. He said unfeelingly, "Maybe it's good the sheriff's dead. Now Ezra can get one of us appointed to his job."

Ezra came pounding towards them from town, leading a horse. Alf began to remove his saddle from the dead horse, and when Ezra led the horse up beside him, he flung it on without waste motion and cinched it down. Gabe said, "All right. Now let's get him."

The eight men spurred away. Miles, grizzled and greying and running to paunch, led off. Gabe fell in behind. After that the others fell in according to age. Alf brought up the rear.

They could still see the fugitive, so it wasn't necessary to trail. He was about a mile or a mile and a half ahead. Mostly the land was flat as a table top, but every once in a while he would disappear into a low spot or a shallow draw. But he always reappeared.

There was a strange matter-of-factness about every one of the pursuing eight. Almost a coldness, as if they were hunting a wolf, as though it were not a human life they were trying to take.

The right or wrong of Spence's killing didn't trouble them, and only in Mart was there any grief. The others pursued this stranger and sought his death simply because when they stuck together nobody dared oppose them. If they ever stopped sticking together, if they failed to avenge Spence's death, then the people in and around Comanche Wells might gain courage from their failure. It was as simple as that, and as uncomplicated.

The few remaining hours of daylight quickly passed. Light faded from the sky. When it was dark, Miles, in the lead, hauled his horse to a halt. "Can't see him no more. Can't trail either."

Gabe waited a moment to see what he would do. When Miles said nothing, he turned to his brothers. "Reckon I'm the best tracker. Ezra and me will camp here for the night. Come mornin', we'll get on the trail. The rest of you keep goin'. Keep ridin' north, same way he was goin' last. If you ain't come up with him by mornin', split into two bunches. Cast around for trail. Maybe you'll find it an' maybe you won't. If you don't, wait for Ezra at Fogarty's roadhouse."

He watched them ride away. Then he

30

dismounted and picketed out his own and Ezra's horses, while Ezra gathered wood for a fire.

Ezra began to prepare supper from rations in the sacks that had been tied behind both his and Gabe's saddles.

Gabe watched him, amusing himself with a comparison between Ezra and a weasel. Ezra was smart, sly and unscrupulous, the only educated one in the family.

A lawyer, the only lawyer for a hundred miles, he had managed, between his sly unscrupulousness and his brothers' ruthlessness, to put together a fair-sized ranch. Trouble was, it wasn't big enough for eight, particularly in these times when the best you could get for a steer was about four dollars, and no takers then.

Ezra was also Justice of the Peace. Gabe grinned to himself. The only justice Ezra dispensed was to the Maxfield family. The only peace the country had was bought at the cost of giving the Maxfields exactly what they wanted.

He ate the beans Ezra handed him and drank two cups of steaming coffee. Then he lay down, pillowed his head on his saddle, and instantly went to sleep.

Several miles to the north, the others

travelled along steadily without pause. It was mostly blind, this nighttime search for the man they sought. It was chancy and probably would not succeed. But it *was* a chance, and the Maxfields took them all.

The hours slipped away, and the long miles fell behind. They rode in silence, a bond between them that made speech unnecessary. They thought alike, wanted the same things. Now they wanted that stranger dead.

Midnight came and passed. Near two in the morning they sighted the dim shape of a stout sod house a quarter mile ahead.

Miles, leading, hauled up and stopped. The others grouped behind him. Will asked, "What do you think, Pa? Reckon he'd of stopped?"

"Might."

"We goin' to ride in an' see?"

"Good idea. Spence hit him twice. He ought to be playin' out."

"Maybe they got him hid."

"Then we'll make 'em tell us where."

They approached in a group. When they were within a hundred feet of the house, Alf, in the rear, and Will, second, peeled off without being told. They dismounted at the rear of the house, left their horses and began to work through the outbuildings.

Miles and the other three rode straight in. Vic and Mart rode around to the side of the house, out of sight of the door, and sat their horses there.

Miles hailed, "Hello the house! Anybody home?"

A lamp went on, visible through the closed shutters, almost at once. A peephole in the stout door darkened briefly, as someone peered out. Then the door opened.

A man stood there in his nightshirt, a rifle in his hands. He boomed in a voice glad for company, any company, "Light down and come on in!"

Miles and Les swung to the ground. They walked towards the door and the man stood back to let them enter. Miles blocked the door until Vic and Mart came up behind him. The four went in, and immediately Les, gun drawn, climbed the ladder to the loft and began to search up there.

The man's face lost its welcoming smile. Alarm touched his calm grey eyes. "What do you want?"

Miles grunted, "Lookin' for a man. Killed one of my sons. Seen him?"

The man's eyes switched appraisingly from Miles to Vic, and on to Mart. They lifted to the loft. They switched to the doorway of another room at the back of the house. He said uncompromisingly, "Get out of here. I wouldn't tell you if I had. You ain't the law."

Miles said, "Vic, go check that room."

The man caught Vic's arm as he started across the room. "My wife's in there. You stay out."

Vic yanked his arm free and started across the room again. The man raised the rifle that was still in his hands.

Miles clipped him, instantly and hard, on the top of the head with the barrel of his revolver. The man grunted heavily and collapsed upon the uneven puncheon floor.

Vic went into the bedroom. There was the sound of a blow, and he staggered back out, the side of his face scraped and beginning to bleed.

Les jumped immediately from the loft and crossed the room at a run. His face was strangely twisted, his eyes unnaturally bright. He licked his lips as he ran.

He jumped into the darkened bedroom, falling and rolling as he went through the door. A woman was briefly visible, swinging a piece of firewood at his head, too late.

She stood exposed in the flickering light for a moment in a long, full nightgown, her black hair tumbling down her back almost to her waist, an uncommonly pretty woman in spite of her disarray.

Les came up behind her and slugged her with his gun. She collapsed, as her husband had, to the puncheon floor, half in and half out of the doorway.

Alf and Will came in. "Nothin' around, Pa. Unless he's in here somewhere."

Les came out of the bedroom. He stood there, looking down at the unconscious woman. Her head was badly cut and she was bleeding profusely.

Miles asked, "Anybody in there, Les?"

Les shook his head.

"Then let's get goin'. I guess he ain't here after all."

The five filed out. All save Les, who stood looking down at the woman, a strange wild look in his eyes.

Miles stuck his head back in the door and said with gentle insistence, "Come on, boy, an' leave her be."

Les looked up. His eyes slowly became more rational. "All right, Pa," he mumbled, and followed reluctantly out the door.

They rode away into the darkness, and had gone several miles before Les was missed. But all Miles said was an irritable, "Damn it, I'll tan that boy when he catches up. I told him to leave her be."

CHAPTER THREE

Luke rode on, hard, for an hour after dark. Then judging the Maxfields would do exactly what they had done, he cut to the west at approximately a forty-five degree angle to the course he had been following.

It wouldn't help him much in the long run, he realized. In the morning they'd pick up his trail and follow it. But it would reduce the chances that they'd overtake him in the darkness and blunder into him by accident.

He was tiring fast now. Loss of blood and pain from the two wounds were beginning to make themselves felt. He knew he couldn't ride all night, knew he'd have to rest.

Accordingly, at midnight, he pulled his horse to a halt beside a trickle of water wandering down a wide, nearly dry stream bed, and let him drink. He got down and without releasing the reins drank deeply himself and refilled his canteen.

He retraced his steps to the grassy side of the stream where there was a thicket of mesquite, and here picketed his horse to graze. There wasn't much chance the horse would stray, but he was taking no chances. No chances at all out here. It was Indian country and a man afoot wouldn't survive.

He forced himself to eat from the sack of provisions the sheriff had tied behind his saddle. Then he lay down and fell into an exhausted, uneasy sleep.

He awoke at dawn and immediately caught his horse and saddled up. Then he ate again, mounted and continued in the same northwesterly direction.

The plain was empty as far as the eye could see — sometimes flat, sometimes rolling, sometimes broken by escarpments of rimrock or by deep, timbered ravines.

He rode warily, a hard and competent man in spite of his wounds and his weakness. His eyes constantly scanned the horizon and the land around. He rode below the crests of the ridges, so that only his head showed along the top.

This way, he covered more than twenty miles before noon and then stopped again to rest both himself and his weary, plodding horse.

Again he ate, knowing he was feverish now, knowing his wounds were festering. Yet he didn't dare remove the bandages. He feared that the pain of removing them would sap his strength to a point where he could not go on.

Damn the Maxfields! How far must he ride before he lost them? How far, before they gave up and turned back? He wished he knew more about them, so that he could assess their probable actions.

During the afternoon, he was not always completely lucid. Memories of the past came flooding to his mind, and sometimes seemed as though they had happened a day or a week before.

On he went, not always in a straight line now. The heat of the sun beat upon him mercilessly. His horse travelled, much of the time, at his own pace, picking his own way. But it was always the same general north-westerly direction, with variations because of the topography of the land.

By late afternoon he could stand no more. He was only half conscious. His head drooped on to his chest. Pain beat through his mind and body like a drum. He had to hole up; he had to rest, or die.

It took him half an hour to picket out his horse. When he had finished, he could stagger no more than a few feet before he fell.

He dropped instantly into a sleep that was close to death. And while he slept the sun dropped to the western horizon and sank behind it. Dusk deepened and became night.

He awoke while it was still dark, feverish and with a terrible, raging thirst. He found his canteen on the ground near his saddle by groping, and took a long, tepid drink from it. He got painfully to his feet and stared around.

He saw nothing, heard nothing save for the noises of the night. He was vaguely hungry and still thirsty and he recognized these things as favourable signs. His wounds were still excruciatingly painful, but for some reason they seemed better than they had last night.

Now he cared — what happened to him, whether the Maxfields found him or not. That, in itself, was a sign of improvement.

Not only did he care . . . His anger was mounting too. Give him time to heal his wounds, give him time to kill this raging fever, and they'd find out they were chasing something besides a rabbit that ran and dodged at every turn. Hunted would turn hunter. He'd make the Maxfield clan wish they'd never heard of him.

It took him a long while to saddle up. By the time he had finished, the sky was turning grey in the east.

He looked ahead at the long miles stretching away to the north. He looked back in the direction he had come. Mounting, he broke into a sweat and turned white. But once he was settled in the saddle it was not so bad. In spite of his fever, he was feeling better, stronger today.

He swung back to a straight northerly course, aware that to continue indefinitely upon his present course would eventually put him into Colorado's high, trackless mountains.

The morning passed. At noon, he ate in his saddle and drank from his canteen. He went on, and in mid-afternoon drew up abruptly as he topped a low escarpment and looked ahead. Buzzards were circling out there, lazily, ominously. Even as he watched, they began to alight.

A dead animal? It was possible, even likely. But the spot was not far off his route and so he turned towards it and rode ahead.

Cautiously. He had seen no tracks, no signs of Indians. Yet he knew this was Comanche country, knew too that he had simply been lucky so far.

Occasionally another buzzard would arrive and settle lazily to the ground. From mere black specks riding the blue air, these slowly grew in size. And then, not a mile away, Luke crossed the trails of several horses.

He halted, his eyes wary and grave. Immediately he reined his horse into a clump of mesquite. He returned on foot to the tracks and studied them.

Six horses had made them — unshod, untrimmed horses. Therefore, he knew they had belonged to Indians, not to the Maxfields.

A hunting or scouting party perhaps. Probably they had killed more game than they could use. Or else the buzzards were feeding on the entrails of a buffalo.

Reassured by the age of the tracks, which he judged were almost half a day old, he returned to his horse, mounted and went on, still in the direction of the feeding carrion birds, and ten minutes later he saw them, walking awkwardly, flapping, quarrelling. In the centre of the clustered birds were two bodies — human bodies.

Luke rode in and the buzzards rose, flapping, thunderously, into the air. They resumed their circling, their shadows like ugly, crawling things upon the ground.

Luke's face twisted. The bodies were those

41

of two men. Both had been scalped, but enough side hair remained on both to tell that one had been grey-haired, the other luxuriantly black-haired. Father and son, Luke supposed. Caught out here alone by that hunting party of braves.

They'd put up quite a fight. The empty paper cartridges around them testified to that. Probably the Indians were lugging one or more of their own party, dead. But they'd triumphed in the end.

The birds had torn the bodies to the extent that it was impossible for Luke to tell if they had been otherwise mutilated by the Indians.

He had seen death before, violent death, yet something about bodies that have been torn to pieces by buzzards . . . Out here, where the sky was so blue, the land so clean, they seemed out of place, their destruction a defiling of an otherwise clean and empty land.

Luke glanced around. He saw nothing move.

He hated the thought of delay, hated too to expend his dwindling strength. But he also hated to leave these men lying here in the sun for the birds to rip and tear and gorge themselves upon.

He looked around for something to dig

with. There was nothing. But a hundred feet away was a dry wash, a cut in the plain made by the erosion of flood.

He walked towards it. It was about six feet deep. Its banks were almost perpendicular and the soil was soft . . .

He returned to the bodies. One by one, closing his mind against the stench they already had, he dragged them to the wash and rolled them in.

He sat down, then, on the bank above them. Bracing his hands and pushing with his heels, he began to crumble off the bank so that the soil rolled down over them.

Exertion made him weak, made his head begin to spin. But he stubbornly continued until he judged he had about a foot and a half of dirt over the bodies.

A damned poor burial, he thought, looking down. The first flood would uncover them and send them tumbling down the wash. But it was the best he could do, the only thing he could do.

Now he walked a circle around the spot where he had found them. He picked up the tracks of the Indian ponies, both coming in and departing. With them as they left had been the horses of the two white men, neither shod, but with the hoof prints showing evidence of recent trimming with nippers and rasp.

He continued his circle until he found the tracks of those same two horses approaching the spot where the pair had died.

Returning to his horse, he mounted. He hesitated between what he knew his responsibility was, and his need to stay ahead of the Maxfield clan.

Whatever family the two dead men had had should be warned. That small party of six braves had happened upon the two men out away from their ranch where they could be killed without too much risk. The ranch itself would be quite another thing. Luke had seen a few of them and knew they were built like forts.

It followed, therefore, that the six braves had gone back for help. And even if they had not, the two men would undoubtedly have womenfolk at their ranch, worrying, wondering. The job of finding out what had happened to them would be all but impossible for women.

Reluctantly, then, he backtracked the horses of the two white men. It was now late, and the sun was sinking rapidly towards the western plain. An hour. Two at most. And then he would be unable to see the trail.

His horse plodded along wearily, his head

hanging. Luke was counting on one thing — the two men probably would not have ridden far from their ranch house.

The sun dropped out of sight, briefly staining the thin clouds a brilliant reddish orange. The clouds faded, by shades of purple and blue, until they were the same dull grey as the darkening sky. It became more and more difficult for Luke to see the trail.

He crossed a narrow, dry wash, rode another hundred yards, and then, suddenly, he saw it.

It was a long house, built of sod. Half buried in the side of a hill, it blended so well with the landscape that if a man didn't know it was there, or wasn't following trail, he could ride right past, particularly in this kind of light.

Heavy wooden shutters protected the narrow windows. A heavy wooden door was strapped with iron.

Beyond the house, connected to it and half hidden by the house itself, was the corral. It held a single horse.

Suddenly, without warning, a rifle boomed from the house, its muzzle shooting out a bright, orange blossom of flame that was quickly obscured by smoke.

Luke left his horse instantly and without

thought. Prone on the ground, he yelled, "Hey! Stop that shooting!"

His head reeled from the pain of his impact with the ground. His horse had trotted only a few weary steps away and now stood dejectedly, head hanging.

No sound came from the house. No light showed. Luke lay still for several moments.

At last he heard a voice, a woman's voice. "What do you want?"

He got to his feet, hands raised. He called, "Some grub if you've got it. A fresh horse if you can spare it."

The same voice said, "Walk this way. Slow. Keep your hands right where they are."

Luke obeyed. The voice sounded young — too young to be the wife of the older man he had found. A daughter, then, or the wife of the younger man.

Her voice hadn't been exactly frightened. Firm rather. Determined. Capable. But that wasn't surprising. A woman would have to be all those things to live out here.

He reached the porch, a long, floorless affair formed by the overhang of the roof timbers and covered with mesquite branches to break the rays of the sun. He stopped immediately before the door.

"What's your name and what are you doing out here alone?"

"Luke Partin, ma'am. I'm headin' north."

"Don't you know this is Comanche country?"

"I know, ma'am."

He heard the bar on the door lift. The heavy door creaked ponderously as it swung open. Luke moved his right hand far enough to remove his hat.

Now the voice was tired. "Come in, Mr. Partin. And welcome."

"Thanks." He stepped inside. The woman closed and barred the door behind him.

There was light in here — only a little from a single lamp turned low. But by its light he could see that she was even younger than he had at first supposed. Nineteen, perhaps, or twenty.

She brushed at her hair with a hand that was brown and strong, an instinctive feminine gesture as old as time itself.

His first impression had been that she was plain. Her face was angular and thin. So, it appeared, was her body beneath the worn, full homespun gown she wore. Her feet were bare.

She crossed the room, got another lamp from a shelf and lighted it. And now he saw her eyes, large and brown and widely spaced. Eyes that didn't go with an angular, barefoot girl in a homespun dress. Looking into those eyes, he realized suddenly that she wasn't plain at all.

He glanced around the room. "You're not alone, are you?"

She eyed him suspiciously, and he realized for the first time how he must look. Sweaty. Dirty, bloody, and stinking of horse and man sweat, and probably from those two bodies too. The girl said, "No, I'm not alone. My father and brother will be coming soon."

Luke's stomach felt empty. Shock touched him. She *was* all alone, now that her men were dead. And he had to be the one to find her, to tell her.

He said, "That's all — your father and brother? No crew?"

She smiled humourlessly. "We did have a crew, but the Comanches chased them off. Usually the Indians stay north of here except for an occasional horse raid. But since last winter when the Cheyennes were wiped out at Sand Creek in Colorado . . . All the tribes are out, making scalp raids now."

Luke said slowly, "I'm afraid they've made one here. I didn't find this place by accident. I backtracked two horses . . ."

Her face drained of blood. Her eyes were, for a moment, stricken with terror.

Luke said quickly, gently, knowing this was the kindest way, "Your father and brother are both dead. I buried them."

She stood there, stunned, for a long, long moment. Luke felt his own weakness beginning to overcome him. He looked around for a chair and headed for it. But he never reached it. Halfway to it he pitched forward and fell, unconscious, to the floor.

CHAPTER FOUR

It was still dark when Luke came to. He was no longer lying on the floor, but had been dragged or carried across the room into one of the smaller rooms at the rear of the house, and raised to the bed.

Pain in his side and arm were greater than before. He was weaker and knew he had lost more blood. Exploring with his hand, he discovered that his bandages had been changed, his clothes removed.

Embarrassment touched him, thinking of the girl doing these things for him, but he realized, too, that keeping busy thus was the best thing she could have done.

He could see the flicker of light through the partly open door and tried to raise up. He managed to make it to a sitting position. Then dizziness overcame him and he was forced to lie down again.

The bed creaked. Immediately the door opened wide and the girl came in, a lamp in her hand. She said sharply, "You'll have to lie still or you'll start those wounds to bleeding again."

Luke didn't reply. He stared at her speculatively, uneasiness touching him now. She was alone and, whether he liked it or not, had become his responsibility. He couldn't leave her here, and damn it, with the time he'd already lost, he hadn't much chance of getting away from the Maxfields if he took her with him.

Her face turned pink and she dropped her glance from his. She said half angrily, "I suppose you've robbed a bank or something and got shot doing it. Are they after you?"

Luke nodded.

"How far behind?"

"Half a day maybe."

Alarm touched her face. "Then you'll have to go on before morning. I can't hide you."

There was gentle mockery in Luke's eyes. "You'd help me get away? Even if I'd robbed a bank?"

Her colour deepened. Luke said, "I didn't rob a bank. I killed a man. His family is after me, and it isn't a trial they've got in mind."

"Then you'll have to go right now. How do you feel?"

Luke lied, "All right, I'll make it."

"I'll saddle a fresh horse for you."

"Mine will do for me. Saddle that one in the corral for yourself."

"I'm not going any place."

Luke tried to sit up again, and this time he made it. He kept the coverlet over him and said irritably, "Damn it, get me some clothes."

There was a hint of amusement briefly in her eyes. She said, "A man isn't exactly a novelty to me, you know. I have . . ."

She stopped. He knew she had been going to say she had a father and brother. But she hadn't. Not any more.

She turned and left the room, biting her lower lip. When she returned, she carried underwear, pants and a shirt. Also a pair of heavy socks.

She laid them on the bed. "Do you need help?"

"I'll manage."

She left the room. Luke stood up, fighting weakness, and got into the underwear. He had to sit down, then, and the creaking of bedsprings drew her call: "Are you all right?"

"Yes."

He waited several moments, then got into the pants, which fit him rather well. He put on the socks, pulled on his boots, and then carefully eased into the shirt.

He buttoned it, still sitting down. Then he got up and walked unsteadily into the main room of the house.

He said, "Haven't you got any shoes?"

"Of course I've got shoes."

"Then put them on."

"Why?"

"Because you can't ride barefooted, damn it! That's why."

"I'm not going any place. I told you that."

Luke forcibly controlled his rising anger. He said patiently, "You can't stay here. That should be plain enough to anyone. Indians just killed your father and brother. Six of them. They rode north, but they'll be back with reinforcements."

Her jaw was set. Her eyes held an almost childish stubbornness.

Luke said, "Indians aren't the only thing. The man I killed had murdered two friends of mine. A man and a woman. He raped their fourteen-year-old daughter and then killed her too. It's his family that's after me. They killed the sheriff in Comanche Wells for trying to help me get away. They're as bad as the one I killed. They're worse than Comanches ever were."

Her face tightened, both with outrage and shock. But she repeated, "I won't go."

"Why, for God's sake? Why? You can't operate this ranch. You can't leave the house. What are you going to do when you run out of supplies? What are you going to do when the Indians come, or the Maxfields?"

She stared at him suspiciously and finally said, "I don't know you. I don't even know you're telling the truth. My father and Ben died for this place, and I won't walk off and leave it. Now go on. Get out of here!"

She was frightened. He could see that. She was almost cold with terror. But she was adamant, too. He knew the only way she'd leave would be if he forced her to.

He stared at her, exasperated. She was strong and wiry for a woman. She would put up a creditable fight. Luke knew he hadn't the strength for subduing her by force. The struggle would undoubtedly start his wounds to bleeding and if that happened, he wouldn't leave at all. He'd be here when the Maxfields came, flat on his back, no help either to himself or to the girl.

He said, "I don't even know your name."

"It's Nancy. Nancy Holcomb. My father was John Holcomb and my brother was named Ben."

He moved a step closer to her, a determined light in his eyes. He wasn't going to leave her here to die and he wasn't going to stay himself. That left him but one alternative. He said, "How do you make a living out here?"

She smiled faintly. "Living? We have a hundred thousand acres and more than ten thousand cattle. But we live off the land — from a patch of corn on the hill behind the house, from the game the land provides and from eating our own beef."

He nodded and took another step without quite meeting her eyes. He was close enough now. He hated to hit her but he didn't know any other way. As it was, catching and saddling the horse in the corral, and lifting her onto it, would tax his strength to its limit.

He looked up as his big hand closed into a fist. His eyes met hers for the briefest instant.

Hers widened with sudden fright. He swung the fist, deeply ashamed even as he did so.

She tried to duck, too late. His fist slammed into the side of her jaw, snapping her head back, driving her body to one side.

He caught her as she fell, wincing and breaking into a sweat as he did. He eased her back into a chair.

She looked smaller now, more helpless. He also realized his first impression that she was gaunt and angular had been wrong. It had been the dress which created that impression. Catching her in his arms had corrected it.

He turned. There was a lantern hanging from a peg beside the door. He lighted it, hating to chance the light outside, but knowing this had to be done quickly.

Taking it down, he carried it outside, closing the door behind.

On the porch, he halted a moment, tensely waiting for the shot that didn't come. Then he crossed the yard purposefully to the corral.

He found a rope hanging from a nail beside the corral gate, and roped the horse quickly by the lantern's light. He led it to a lean-to at one side of the house, where he found a woman's sidesaddle and a horsehair pad.

He saddled the horse quickly, afterwards leading it to the door, where his own horse still stood listlessly. It would be better if he had a fresh one, but since he hadn't, he'd have to make the best of this one.

He went in. Still carrying the lantern he went into the small room that was her bedroom and gathered up some things he thought she might want or need. It embarrassed him to be going through her things, but at last he finished and returned to the big main room.

She still slumped, unconscious, in the chair. Gritting his teeth against the pain, he lifted her, carried her outside, and laid her face down across the saddle. He wrapped her ankles well to protect them from rope burns, did likewise with her wrists. Then he roped them together under the horse's belly so that she would not slide off.

He had to grin to himself, as he thought of her anger when she came to. She'd hate him for as long as she lived. But she would live, and that was more than she'd do if he left her here.

He went back into the house, poured water on the fire and blew out the lamps, one by one. He doubted if this house would last long with no one to guard it. Comanches would burn it as soon as they discovered it was unoccupied. The cattle would roam, wild and free, until someone discovered them and decided to help themselves.

And yet, this would happen no matter what Luke did. The only difference was, if he left the girl she'd be dead when the ranch went to pot. This way, perhaps she could return, rebuild, gather up what was left. She might marry, or she might recruit a crew.

He closed the door, dropping the bar into

place by means of the rawhide latchstring. Then he picked up the reins of Nancy Holcomb's horse, mounted, and rode away towards the north.

The sky was greying in the east. Luke was weak and tired and full of pain, but he clenched his jaws and forced his horse into a sluggish, reluctant trot.

It revolved, now, on whether the Maxfields were able to obtain fresh horses. It was likely that they would. With eight of them to help, they could round up and catch the first bunch of loose horses they came upon. Probably today.

After that, it would only be a matter of hours.

The land was changing and was no longer flat. Now, it was cut by deep, timbered ravines, by high, rocky plateaux upon which scrub cedars and piñon grew. There was cover for a man, but there was also cover for lurking Indians to ambush him.

The sun came up, immediately scorching hot. Heat waves rose shimmering into the cool morning air.

Luke plodded on, beginning now to become concerned about the girl. Had he struck her too hard? Had he hurt her beyond the hurt of knocking her out?

In the shelter of a deep ravine, he halted

his horse and dismounted. He walked back to where Nancy Holcomb still lay, unmoving, upon her horse. He untied her hands and feet, not noticing that her eyes were open and watching him with furious, smouldering hatred.

As soon as the ropes were off, she doubled her legs and kicked savagely.

Her feet, still bare, struck him full in the chest, driving him back and away. He fell flat on his back, his wind knocked out, and lay there for a moment, gasping for breath.

Nancy slid off the horse. Spread-legged, she glared down at him, her hair in complete disarray and hanging almost to her waist.

She looked completely wild, fierce. She said angrily, "Damn you! Oh damn you!"

Luke got his breath. His face was grey, and he could feel the two wounds, warm and wet again. Damn this girl anyway! Between her trying to help him and trying to hurt him, she had him so blasted weak he could hardly stand, let alone mount a horse and ride. He got up and stood there swaying, wanting to grin but not daring, wanting too to rage at her, to knock some sense into her pretty, stubborn head.

He said, "I should have left you there. I should have left you for the Comanches or the Maxfields, whoever got there first."

"I just wish you had. Nobody asked you to come butting in."

"What the hell's the matter with you? Do you *want* to die?"

"Nobody's going to die. Unless it's you. And I wish you would."

Luke said, "Get on that horse." His eyes were cold. This might have been funny under other circumstances. In hostile Comanche country, with the Maxfields maybe only hours behind, it was certainly not.

She said, "I won't. You can't make me."

"No. I guess I can't. But I can leave you here. And I will, if you don't get on that horse right now!"

He picked up the reins of Nancy's horse, walked to his own. He put a foot in the stirrup, seized the horn with his right hand and tried to swing astride.

Pain turned his face grey. For a moment, the world went black. Furiously, he tried again, and this time made it up.

His head hung forward and he could scarcely see. He looked in Nancy's direction. Her face was blurred before his eyes, and so he did not see the odd contradiction of expression there. He croaked, "Coming?"

He thought she would stamp her foot, bare, against the rocky ground, so great was her rage. She said, "I'll get even with you!"

60

"Are you coming?" he shouted.

"Yes. I'm coming. But you're going to wish I hadn't."

He shrugged faintly. He waited until she had mounted, then tied the reins of her horse to his saddle horn so that she couldn't pull away.

"There's shoes in that bundle tied behind your saddle. And some other things I thought you'd need."

She didn't reply, nor did Luke look back. But later, when he glanced behind, he saw that she had them on, black, high-button shoes.

On and on they went, into the uninhabited land ahead where only savages roamed, and where white men went at the risk of their lives. The hours dragged for Luke, fighting always his increasing weakness.

They ate sparingly at noon, stopped twice to refill canteens. And went on through the blistering heat.

At last, two hours before sundown, Luke knew that he could not go on. Maxfields or no Maxfields, he had reached the limit of his strength.

CHAPTER FIVE

They made camp in a shallow ravine, at the bottom of which a small stream ran. Luke collapsed to the ground immediately, closing his eyes. He was breathing heavily and his head was whirling. If only Spence Maxfield had been a poorer shot he might have made it all right with only one wound. Two were more than he could take and still remain strong.

He heard Nancy Holcomb moving about, and opened his eyes to look at her. She was picketing the horses. When she had finished, she returned and began to gather wood. Luke said, "No fire."

She gave him a smouldering, angry look, but she stopped gathering wood. Luke rested for about ten minutes and then sat up.

He was facing something in his mind, however reluctantly. He was beat. He couldn't hope to outdistance the Maxfields.

He couldn't hope to stay ahead of them more than another day at most.

There were several things he could do, not one of them palatable. He could send the girl on, alone, provided she would go. He could give her the fresh horse and pray to God she'd make it through. But it was unlikely that she would — in fact, it was virtually impossible.

The second alternative was even less palatable than the first, and entirely foreign to Luke's nature. This was to take the fresh horse himself, leave the girl to return home if she could on his own, worn-out horse.

The third alternative was the one he finally decided on. It was to find a spot someplace from which he could fight, and hole up there until he was strong again. The success of this plan depended largely on luck, on the chance that the Maxfields had lost the trail, or that they had given up, or that he could successfully fight them off if they did find him.

Accordingly, he got painfully to his feet, caught the fresh horse that had been in the Holcomb corral, saddled and mounted. Nancy looked at him with hostile, inquiring eyes. He said, "We've got to hole up. I'll look for a place. Don't get any ideas about running off. I can catch that played-out horse in less than an hour even if you do."

She didn't reply. Her eyes hated him silently. But he saw something else in her as well — terror, uncertainty, the panic that comes from being orphaned and left alone, from being uprooted and yanked from all that was familiar and safe and dear.

He wanted to comfort and reassure her, but he knew it was impossible. She didn't trust him. She didn't even like him. And she'd accept no comfort from him.

He rode away, climbing the slope of the ravine.

He came out, glanced instinctively south, then searched all the horizons for dust or movement. He saw nothing.

He angled along the crest of the ridge, his eyes inspecting the land critically. Over there, five miles or more away, was an escarpment. Up there might be a cave or a pile of rocks that would offer shelter. He was familiar with land like this, and knew that erosion often carves out overhangs in the soft sandstone rims.

Water, and feed for the horses, would be the problem. To find all these things in one place was more than he had a right to hope for. But if he could find at least shelter, a place he could defend . . .

He rode steadily towards the distant rim.

By the time he reached it, the sun was settling behind the western horizon.

He put his horse up the steep, shaly slope. Water he would not find; he knew that now. Not high against that rim. Nor would he find feed for the horses. They'd have to picket the horses some distance away.

He found the spot he sought almost immediately. It was a deeply eroded overhang, perhaps a dozen feet in depth. It faced west, and would inevitably become an oven in late afternoon. It was an oven now. But immediately before it was a jumble of rocks broken off the rim above in ages past, which provided shelter from below. A couple of these rocks were large enough to offer shade from the late afternoon sun.

He rode his horse as close as he could, then dismounted to inspect the place. At one spot there was a build-up of alkali on the face of the rock wall, indicating that water had once seeped through, but now it was dry as a bone.

Luke returned to his horse and mounted. If he hurried they could reach this place before full dark.

He returned along the way he had come, and in the grey of dusk reached the place where he had left the girl.

She was waiting for him, sitting dejectedly

on a rock staring at the ground. She looked up in quick fright when she heard his horse. Then her face settled into its familiar expression of dislike.

He said, "I've found a place. Saddle up and come on."

"What if I won't?"

"Then I'll leave you here. Alone."

She stayed stubbornly on the rock. Luke reined away. Immediately she got up and hurried towards Luke's picketed horse.

The faintest of smiles touched his wide, grim mouth. But it was not a mocking smile; it was one of understanding and pity.

She saddled his horse and mounted stiffly. Luke led out and she followed, her eyes resting upon his back, smouldering.

Dark came down before they reached the place, but he had marked its location well in his mind and found it without difficulty. When they reached it, he said, "Get down. Wait for me."

She dismounted silently and stood, unmoving, in the dark mouth of the natural cave. Luke reined over and rode along the foot of the rim for almost a mile before he found a way out on top.

He climbed the rocky trail, his horses scrambling frantically for footing. Reaching the top, he rode blindly for about a quarter mile until he found a low spot, one that would probably not be visible from the land around. There was no water. A trip would have to be made each day to change the picket stakes and water the horses. Until the Maxfields came.

He picketed the horses out and hid the saddles and bridles in a clump of brush. Then, carrying his canteen and the sack of grub, as well as the sack of Nancy's personal things, he retraced his steps slowly.

The mile and a quarter he had come now seemed like ten afoot. It took nearly an hour to cover it. When he reached the overhang, he tossed down the sacks and the canteen and sagged to the ground. He said, "Get something to eat out of that sack. Go easy on the water. It's all we've got."

Apparently she found a can of beans and a can opener in the sack. She brought him the can and he ate half of it, cold, by shovelling it into his mouth with his knife. He took a drink from the canteen.

Nancy began to eat the remainder of the beans. When she had finished she asked, "What do you think you're going to do, hide here from them? What are we going to eat? And what about water?"

He stared at her dim shape patiently. "I haven't any choice. I've got to stop and rest.

As slow as we've been travelling, they'd catch us anyway before long. This way, maybe I'll be in shape to fight them off."

"And what about me?"

He said, "What about you? It looks like we're stuck with each other whether we like it or not, so we might as well be as pleasant about it as possible."

"Do you realize what you've made me abandon?"

"A hundred thousand acres. Ten thousand cattle. They aren't going to run away. You can come back. But if you'd stayed you'd have been dead inside a week, or a captive in some Comanche buck's tepee, or a plaything for the Maxfield clan."

She was silent. He couldn't see her face, but he supposed that had shocked her. He didn't care. She needed shocking. Maybe then she'd get over the notion of wanting to go back.

He lay down and stared at the stars in the flawless, cloudless sky. Nancy Holcomb sat hunched against the rim, hugging her knees. He felt a surge of pity for her. She was alone and scared. She'd had to bear the loss of her father and brother without comfort, without solace. She hadn't been able to bury them properly, even.

Her voice was low, soft in the darkness.

"Was it hard for them, Mr. Partin? Or did they die quickly?"

He said, "They died instantly, from gunshot wounds. There was probably little or no pain, little or no time to realize they were leaving you alone. Why were they out there anyway?"

"They went out to butcher a steer. We were out of meat. Usually only one of them went out at a time and the other stayed with me. But butchering is a two-man job."

Luke didn't answer. It was a two-man job if you wanted to save all the meat. But with ten thousand cattle . . . they'd have been better off to send one man out and just cut off a hindquarter.

He felt himself drowsing, slipping from full consciousness into a half world of sleep.

She snapped him out of it with her sudden question, "Are the horses all right? Where did you leave them?"

He said drowsily, "Up on top. There's a trail about a mile north."

He went back to sleep. Once he dreamed she was crying, and woke fitfully, half delirious. She *was* crying, softly and to herself. It was like listening to a child cry, its face buried in a pillow. It twisted his heart and made him ashamed for his harshness towards her.

But he didn't get up. Better to let her have it out, tonight. Better to let her cry all the grief and loneliness out.

Again sleep that was near to unconsciousness took him.

He awoke as the first grey of dawn began to stain the sky, aware of a deep feeling of uneasiness. He sat up instantly and looked around. He was alone.

He got to his feet stiffly, clenching his jaws against the pain in his wounds, which had scabbed and stopped bleeding during the night. He walked to the edge of the overhang and stared out across the plain.

No dust. No movement. But he stood there motionless for nearly five minutes, examining each section of it with minute care.

Satisfied then, he turned north and walked a dozen steps along the foot of the rim.

There were the tracks of her high-button shoes, plain and unmistakable in the soft ground. And the tracks were fresh. Perhaps he could catch her before she found the horses . . .

He returned to the cave and snatched up the canteen. Damn her! Now he had to expend badly needed strength climbing that rim.

He walked along. He began to sweat, both

from pain and from exertion. He began to grow weaker.

And then, from a distance of half a mile, he saw her ride down the rimrock trail and head down the slope towards the level land below.

She looked up from the foot of the slope, saw him and raised a hand. Then she rode away, diminishing steadily in size until she went out of sight into the draw where they had first stopped last night.

Luke sat down. She had left him a horse, but the animal must be watered and moved each day. Doing this would take every bit of Luke's strength and delay his recovery from his wounds.

A feeling of hopelessness touched him, soon replaced by furious, raging anger. Damn them, they wouldn't beat him even before they arrived. He'd return to the cave and rest, and watch, and wait. When they came he'd be ready. Killing him wouldn't be cheap for them.

He got up and retraced his steps to the cave. He wet his lips from the canteen, then corked it and slumped to the rocky floor.

Perhaps the girl would make it back and perhaps she would not. He hadn't the strength to follow her and find out. To try would only be to die out on the empty plain.

CHAPTER SIX

Riding away, Nancy Holcomb glanced up at the foot of the rim and saw Luke watching her. She raised a hand, then dropped it abruptly and turned her face away.

She hated him. He was brutal and savage and had probably lied about the man he had killed and about those who were following him.

And yet, if she hated him, why did she feel such shame at leaving him thus? Why did she feel like weeping all over again, just as she had last night?

She pulled her thoughts forcibly away from Luke. She needn't worry about him. He still had his horse and saddle, his gun. He was better off than when he'd come to her — his wounds were clean and would heal, given the chance. He was tough and competent and only needed time.

Worry about what was ahead, she told herself. Worry about being alone in the sod house surrounded by a million square miles of hostile land.

She'd have to leave, and soon. She'd have to ride south to Comanche Wells and try to recruit a crew. Perhaps the Maxfields could spare a man or two to ride with her . . .

There was gold hidden under the puncheon floor — enough to pay a good-sized crew for several months. And there were rumours of a cattle market in Kansas.

She kicked the horse with her heels and he loped ahead. The sun came up, again blistering hot in a cloudless sky. What would she do, she wondered, if she met a hunting party of Comanches? Run, she supposed. Hope her horse could outdistance their short-legged ponies. Because she didn't even have a gun.

The morning hours passed. Once she saw a cloud of dust to northward. It seemed to be moving towards the southeast.

Indians. She knew this land and knew its ways. Not for nothing had she been raised out here.

Thereafter, she kept to the low spots so that the dust of her horse's passage would not show. And rode with quiet panic in her brown eyes, glancing continually to right and left and often behind.

Growing in her was a kind of sustained

terror, born of her knowledge that she was wholly unable to cope with the situation into which life had thrust her. And this feeling was accentuated by a feeling of terrible aloneness.

Grief was dulled before terror. But grief still crouched in the back of her mind.

She would welcome sight of the Maxfields now. They were white men, men of her kind, as Ben and her father had been. They wouldn't hurt her. Luke had been lying about that. He was assuming that they were like the Maxfield he had killed, and he had no logical basis for such a belief.

All morning she travelled; she guessed she covered more than twenty miles. She rode ever south, knowing she would recognize landmarks as soon as she came within a dozen miles of her home.

She did begin to recognize them in early afternoon, and thereafter laid a direct course for the house. And then she began to worry. What, if, during her absence, the Comanches had come and found the house unoccupied, undefended? It would be a heap of charred rubble when she found it.

She squinted her eyes, searching the spot where the house should be below the horizon for a wisp of smoke. She saw nothing.

She breathed a little easier, but she did

not relax the hard pace at which she drove her horse.

Half a dozen miles. Then she would top a long, low rise and see it below her . . .

Her eye caught movement to her right. Glancing that way fearfully, she saw an Indian ride into sight out of a shallow ravine. He was followed immediately by a second, and a third.

He hadn't seen her yet. For an instant, pure panic ruled her thoughts. The Indians were less than half a mile away.

Should she dismount and try to remain motionless in the hope they would miss her? There wasn't a bit of cover for more than a quarter mile. Or should she run for it?

Forcing calm to her agitated mind, she calculated the course the Indians were following. It was a quartering one and would come within less than an eighth of a mile of where she was.

But if she ran, she could probably beat them to the house.

She hesitated for the barest instant. And the Indians made the decision for her. The second one in line saw her, raised an arm to point. Then all three wheeled their horses towards her in a run.

Nancy drummed on her horse's ribs with her heels. She wished she didn't have this awkward sidesaddle. It was a bit ridiculous to have your life jeopardized because of society's code of propriety.

Still, she was expert, on this kind of saddle, or any other, or none at all. Leaning low over the horse's withers, her skirts whipping out behind her, she pounded towards the south, with the Indians now less than an eighth of a mile behind.

Their cries were wild, shrill, exultant. Something cold began to grow in Nancy's spine and spread throughout her body until it was like ice. She began to tremble, and however she fought against it, her trembling increased.

If the house was destroyed she was doomed. She accepted that. Even if it was not destroyed, she was probably doomed. She might delay her capture or death by an hour or two. But one lone woman couldn't hope to fight off a determined trio of Indians for very long.

They gained on her steadily, and as they did, her terror increased. They were not shooting at her, though they were within rifle range. That meant but one thing to her. They wanted her alive. She shuddered at the implications of that. She drummed upon her horse's sides with the heels of her high-button shoes, urging him to greater speed.

Strange what slight things affected the course of a person's life. Without the shoes, she wouldn't have had a chance. She knew this horse and had ridden him often. He would have paid no attention at all to the drumming of her bare heels upon his sides. So, indirectly, by bringing along her shoes, Luke had saved her life.

Closer and closer the Indians came until, looking behind, she could see their faces, see the eager, savage looks upon them. She could make out the details of their accoutrements, could see each individual streak of paint upon their faces.

And then, at last, she saw the house ahead. She pounded down the slope with the Indians now less than a hundred yards behind.

She dismounted, running, her skirts lifted almost to her knees so that she wouldn't trip. She realized with but a part of her mind that the corral was full of horses. And then she heard the boom of rifles from the high and narrow windows, and saw the puffs of smoke.

The Indians, realizing at once that their hope of capturing her was gone, immediately opened up on her. A bullet ticked her sleeve. Another slammed into the doorjamb beside her as she plunged through the suddenly opened door.

It slammed behind her and she heard a harsh voice, "Got two of 'em. Get that other bastard before he gets away!"

The room was filled with powder smoke. It was filled with something else — the smell of many unwashed men.

The Maxfields. They were here. And they had saved Nancy's life in spite of Luke's dire predictions.

One of them yelled, "Got the bastard, Gabe!"

They rushed to the door and spilled out into the yard. As though directed by someone, they paired off, two going to each of the Indians.

One of each pair stood back, gun ready and pointed at the still form, while the other moved in, knife in hand.

Nancy turned away from the door. Behind her she heard someone say, "Leave those goddam scalps outside. There's a lady here. You want to make her sick?"

Someone out in the yard guffawed. Nancy sank weakly into a chair.

She wasn't blind. She had seen their faces; she had smelled their unwashed smell; she had looked at their eyes . . .

A tiny shiver of fear touched her. Luke Partin had said they were worse than Comanches. Now she was beginning to wonder if what he had said weren't true.

They trooped into the house, some of them wiping bloody hands on the fronts of their filthy pants legs. They looked at her in the way a hungry dog looks at a side of beef. They licked their heavy lips and ran hands over their whiskered faces.

The two who had remained in the doorway while the others finished off and scalped the Indians now drew her glance. One was obviously the father. He was past sixty and his face was seamed, his hair almost white. The other appeared to be about forty, and was also greying over the ears.

This one glanced at his father, waited a moment and then turned to her. He said, "I'm Gabe Maxfield, ma'am. This here's my Pa, and these others are my brothers. I take it you live here."

She nodded dumbly.

"Then those two we found that the buzzards had been at must've been your menfolks. You all alone now?"

She wanted to lie, but she knew it would do no good. She hadn't fooled Luke Partin and she certainly wouldn't fool the Maxfields. She nodded again.

"Where you been?"

She lied quickly, "Looking for my father

and brother."

One of the others said, "She's lyin', Gabe."

"Shut up." He stared at her, his eyes running up and down her body. "You *are* lyin', ma'am. You know it an' I know it. Now I'm goin' to tell you somethin'. We'll all get along just fine if you tell us the truth. Now again. Where you been?"

"Looking for my father and brother, I tell you. I don't believe you when you say they're dead. They can't be!"

Gabe said, "I'll give you one more chance. But before I ask you this time, I'll tell you what we already know. Luke Partin's been here. We trailed him here. That's how we found the bodies of your menfolk. We know somethin' else. Your menfolks have been dead nigh on to three days an' nights. You been gone for two. You rode outa here with Luke Partin and you rode back in alone. Now what we want to know is where did you leave him? An' how bad is he hurt?"

Nancy didn't speak. Gabe waited patiently. One of the others, a thin-faced, powerful man nearly six feet tall, said, "I can make her talk up, Gabe. Just lemme . . ."

The father spoke. "You got a tannin' comin' for what you done back at the last place we stopped. You shut up, or I'll give it to you now."

Gabe said quietly, "Les likes to see things hurt. But don't you worry none, ma'am. All you got to do is speak right up."

She looked from Gabe to Les. Les had tiny, close-set black eyes and teeth that protruded slightly. His eyes were bright now. He was sweating. And he was nervously wetting his lips with his tongue.

She shuddered visibly. Gabe grinned at her and then at Les. "You give her the shivers, Les."

He looked back at Nancy, mockery in his eyes. "I could let Les take you out behind the corral for a while. But I got me a better idea. I think I'll just take all the clothes off you and let you run around nekkid. You can cook an' keep house for us, but without a stitch on you." He was grinning widely now and turned to look at his brothers. "How's that sound, boys? You could look all you pleased but you couldn't touch. Not unless she still wouldn't talk."

Nancy felt weak. She felt as though her blood had turned to ice water. Frozen in her chair, she could not have moved no matter how she tried.

If only she'd listened to Luke! If only she'd believed! All the things he'd said about the Maxfields were true. They were worse, even, than Luke had said they were.

81

Every one of the eight were staring at her now, eyes bright, faces flushed and shiny with sweat. She imagined herself living around the eight of them without any clothes to cover her . . .

A dull flush began at her neck and spread over her face.

Gabe chuckled. "A fair trade, ma'am. You keep your clothes and tell us what we want to know."

She stared at him helplessly, pleading with her eyes. He only grinned more widely.

She thought of Luke Partin, hidden in that cave thirty miles north of here. They'd find him eventually by tracking anyway. So what harm would it do to tell? She couldn't give them exact directions anyway. With her directions they'd probably find Luke no less soon than they would all by themselves.

And if she did tell them, they'd go away at once.

Or would they? She opened her mouth to speak, but no sound came out.

Gabe's voice was gentle, exaggeratedly so. "Now ma'am, don't you be so scared. I told the boys they couldn't touch. An' I'll watch real close to see they don't. That is, if I'm here. Only I just might be the one that has to go after Partin, seein' as how I'm the best tracker."

Anger was beginning to rise in Nancy. It drove away some of the fear. She said, her voice surprisingly strong under the circumstances, "I can't tell you. He forced me to go with him, and he took me north. For a whole day. Early this morning I got away from him, took one of the horses and came home."

"Then he must be hurt pretty bad if he couldn't stop you from getting away."

"He was sleeping."

"How come you was so anxious to come back? You knowed you didn't have no menfolks to look after you. You got gold hid out around here, someplace?"

She looked away, knowing her eyes would betray the truth. She shook her head. One of the brothers yelped, "By God she has! Make 'er tell us where, Gabe!"

"You shut up, Alf. I'll take care of this." He stared at Nancy speculatively. "Was it gold, ma'am, or was it just this place?"

She said weakly, "This place. It's home."

"Sure it is." He clucked sympathetically. "Sure it's home. How big is it, ma'am?"

He seemed able to almost read her mind. He seemed to know instinctively just the things she wished to hide. A feeling of utter helplessness began to possess her. She would be better off if she had been killed along with her father and Ben. Or a while ago, by those three Comanches. She had a sudden, hopeless feeling that what lay ahead for her would be infinitely worse.

CHAPTER SEVEN

Nancy Holcomb stared around at their faces, at Alf, whose face was covered with boils under his untidy fuzz of whiskers, at Ezra, whose face was as pointed as a weasel's, at Les, whose eyes made her stomach churn.

She said weakly, "It's a hundred thousand acres."

Gabe whistled soundlessly. "How many cattle?"

"I don't know," she said helplessly. "I don't know."

"You've got to know. You lived here, didn't you? Les, get her dress off her, for a start."

Les grinned and took a step towards her.

Nancy said quickly, breathlessly, "Ten thousand."

Again Gabe whistled soundlessly. He glanced around at his brothers. "Say now, we got to treat this girl with more respect. She's an heiress. She's got a hundred thousand acres and ten thousand cattle. And gold hid someplace around. We can't treat her like any old girl livin' in a shack."

Les looked disappointed. So did the others. The old man, Miles, looked on impassively.

Gabe stared at Nancy until she could no longer meet his eyes. He asked, "What kind of title you got? Squatters claim?"

"It's a land grant. A Spanish land grant."

Gabe chuckled. "Hear that, boys? She owns it, lock stock and barrel. We oughtta thank Luke Partin for killin' Spence. Looky what it got us."

Les complained, "Hell, *she* owns it, Gabe. Not us."

Gabe said, "Shut up. You think I haven't thought of that? Alf, you're about her age, ain't you? How'd you like to have her?"

Alf began to grin sheepishly. He looked around from one to the other of his brothers. "Right now?"

"Nah. I don't mean like that. I mean for a wife. How'd you like to marry her? Ezra's a justice of the peace. He can marry you. All legal and everything. Then you'll own this place an' all them cattle. An' have the girl to boot. How'd that be, Alf? Pretty nice, huh?"

"You're funnin' me." Alf was faintly

flushed with anger and confusion.

Gabe said, "I ain't funnin', Alf. I ain't funnin' at all. Course, if we fixed it up so you owned all this an' her too, you wouldn't be stingy about it, would you? There's eight of us. Pa an' me an' Ezra, why we'd be satisfied with just the gold. We'd go on back home. The place back there will take care of three of us real well. Besides that, you'd need help to run this place an' we'd just as well keep it in the family. Will an' Vic an' Mart an' Les could stay on to help you. For a share."

"I reckon that'd be all right."

"Sure it would. A fifth of what the place earns for each of you. An' you keep the girl for yourself. That is unless you want to share her once in a while too."

Nancy stared at Gabe in complete disbelief. What he was proposing was monstrous. And she would have no more to say about it than a captive or a slave.

This was impossible! It couldn't be happening. It was a bad dream, a nightmare, from which she must soon awake. When she did she would find that Luke Partin had been a myth, that her father and Ben were still alive. These men were something conjured up out of a dreaming mind, and would go away as soon as she awoke.

Looking around her, she knew it was no dream. It was real, and these men were real too, however incredible they seemed. Luke hadn't lied about them. They were worse than Comanches.

Gabe said, "First, though, we got us a job. We got to get that killer, Luke Partin. We got to take what's left of him back to Comanche Wells. After all, he did kill Spence — an' the sheriff too. He's got to pay."

Alf had been watching Nancy steadily. Occasionally he would lick his lips. His face was flushed and sweating. The boils stood out angrily. When she glanced at him, he'd look away. But when her eyes left him, he would resume his hungry staring.

Gabe said, "Come on, Les. You too, Mart. We'll go get Partin. If we leave right now we ought to be back in a couple of days."

Alf cleared his throat. Still looking at Nancy he said, "Couldn't you have Ezra marry us right now?"

Gabe shouted with laughter. The others joined. Alf's face grew even redder. Sweat poured off his temples and down his cheeks. He said, "Aw, cut it out. I only thought . . ."

Gabe roared, "We know what you thought, Alf! But nothin' doin'. Still, I admire you, boy. I didn't think you had it in you."

The laughter died gradually.

Gabe stepped towards the door. "Get the horses, Les. Mart, you stir up some rations."

He turned. "Alf, you be real nice to her while we're gone. Court her, like. We don't want her to feel like she ain't had all a girl's got a right to expect. We don't want her to feel we're rushin' her into this."

Nancy stared up at him. She couldn't tell whether he was being sarcastic or whether he meant what he said.

She'd *have* to get away, escape. Tonight, maybe, while they were all asleep. If she could get out, and to the corral . . .

She'd face the Comanches now, gladly. If she had to. She'd take her chances alone out on the plain. Even death would be preferable to what the Maxfields had in mind for her — a lifetime of virtual slavery at the whims of Alf and his brothers.

Gabe stepped out through the door. Immediately he turned back irritably. "Damn it, does everybody have to be told what to do? Some of you get out of here and get rid of these damn stinkin' Injuns. The lady don't want a bunch of spoiled meat litterin' up her front yard and neither does Alf. Do you, Alf?"

Alf grumbled something indistinguishable. He got up and went outside. The others followed. Nancy stayed where she was. She heard Gabe yell from the door, "Vic, strip them Injun ponies an' turn 'em loose. Bury the gear with the bodies."

Then Gabe was standing in the doorway staring at her. There was no respect on his face and no levity in his voice. His eyes were hard as ice. "Don't you get no ideas into your pretty head about gettin' away, missy. Try it an' I'll see you get a taste of the quirt. Understand?"

Nancy nodded dumbly. He couldn't threaten her with anything worse than what he had promised as a certainty. Marriage to Alf! She shuddered.

No, threats wouldn't deter her efforts to try and escape. But a feeling of hopelessness crept over her in spite of her determination not to let it do so. She was one lone girl against eight ruthless men, and the chances were a thousand to one that she'd never be able to escape.

All that morning Luke Partin lay in the overhang beneath the rim. He slept fitfully, off and on. Whenever he awoke, he would crawl painfully to a spot from which he could see the plain below. Then, when he had satisfied himself that no one was approaching, he would crawl back.

He cursed his weakness and damned his helplessness. It did no good, nor did he expect it to. Healing was a matter of time, and he would have to be patient.

If the girl had stayed, he'd have mended sooner. True, he had food enough and water enough to last a couple of days. But sometime this evening, after it cooled down, he would have to climb the rim to where he'd left his horse. He'd have to ride the animal to water, and then picket him in a new place. He wouldn't be able to avoid leaving a trail.

Indians, if they happened upon the horse or upon his tracks, would know someone was around. They'd wait, and ambush him when he came.

Luke shrugged fatalistically. He had a feeling he wouldn't get out of this alive. He didn't honestly see how he could. Too much was against him. The Maxfields. The hostile land, teeming with Comanches who were out for scalps. His wounds, which would prevent the kind of defence he would normally have been able to put up.

But he promised himself one thing — they wouldn't catch him by surprise. Indians or the Maxfields, he'd make them know there had been a fight.

When the sun came around to the west

and began to beat into the cave, he crawled out and lay in the shade of one of the big sandstone rocks. The heat increased. He sweated profusely and grew thirstier by the hour. But he didn't take a drink. Taking one now would only make him sweat more, and make him need a drink more. If he waited until evening, one sparing drink would do. He couldn't be sure he'd make it to the stream.

The land lay before him empty and baking in the afternoon sun. It looked peaceful and serene. It was beautiful in its way, and Luke lay there drinking it in.

He loved the semi-arid land, loved its heat and sudden storms. He could understand the implacable way the Comanches fought to hold it against the infiltrating tide of whites.

It was a good land. Someday it would be settled. There would be towns and fences and roads and even schools. For those who settled it now and fought to hold what they had gained there would be peace and plenty.

He grinned wryly to himself. Right now the odds that he'd be one of these were poor and getting poorer. Nancy Holcomb, if she hadn't run into Indians, should be home by now, Luke was willing to bet that she'd either encountered the Maxfields on the way or found them already there when she'd reached the house. Either way, they'd be along tomorrow. If they were anything like Spence they wouldn't care how they got information out of Nancy. But get it they would. They'd probably make her tell exactly where Luke was.

He wouldn't blame her if she told. He didn't expect a girl to hold out against a bunch like the Maxfields. And anyway, the greatest difference it could make would be three or four hours. They'd have found him, with or without Nancy's information.

But what would they do with her when Luke was dead? That question bothered him. Would they treat her as Spence had treated Miguel Ortiz's daughter, or would they escort her back to the safety of Comanche Wells?

The sun sank slowly out of sight in the west. The heat lessened and the grey of early dusk swept across the land.

Luke struggled to his feet. He searched the land again and, finding it empty, picked up his canteen and hobbled along the foot of the rim towards the trail.

It was darkening fast, but he reached it and climbed out to the top. He found his horse, mounted and rode back down the trail.

He slid down the talus slope in early darkness and rode the five miles to the stream beside which he had camped with Nancy. He watered his horse, drank deeply himself and refilled his canteen. Then he rode back. He picketed his horse near the spot he had before and returned to the cave.

It was late when he arrived. He flopped to the ground in exhaustion and closed his eyes. Tomorrow was, he knew, the fateful day. Tomorrow would decide whether he was to live or die.

CHAPTER EIGHT

Gabe and Les and Mart rode north of the ranch buildings for half a mile. Then Gabe said shortly, "All right. Fan out and pick up his trail. It'll be two horses, his an' hers."

He halted his horse and watched his brothers work. One rode left, the other right. They rode at a walk, their eyes on the ground. They were good, and it would only be a matter of minutes before one of them picked up Partin's trail. He waited patiently, feeling a kind of possessive pride in his two brothers, but feeling too that something was lacking.

Always before, the Maxfield clan had been self-sufficient, and Gabe had felt strong pride in their self-sufficiency. But something about that girl had stirred him to the vaguest kind of discontent.

Suddenly he wanted more than the boar's nest back near Comanche Wells. He wanted more than the animal-like existence there, wanted someone besides his animalistic brothers for companions.

He scowled, vaguely ashamed of his thoughts. He was the head of the clan. What kind of thoughts were these?

Maybe they did have some rough edges. That was natural enough. They'd never really had a mother — not since they were small at least, and she'd been too busy then with new babies to pay much attention to the ones that were past the helpless stage.

Gabe remembered her, a quietly hopeless woman, growing thinner and weaker with each new child, getting behind a little more each day with the washing, the cooking, the sewing, the cleaning, until one by one those chores were dropped, until little by little the place deteriorated from a woman's house, kept that way, to the boar's nest it was now, strictly utilitarian, and for men only.

She died bearing Alf, and Miles rode to town immediately after she was put into the ground, coming back with a fat, slovenly Indian woman who would cook and nothing else, but who had large fruitful breasts that Alf could share with her dark-skinned baby whose father she couldn't even name.

She was no substitute for the mother they had known. She gave no thought to anything but their animalistic needs — food, a place to sleep . . . and later she took them to bed with her as unquestioningly as a sow takes a boar, regardless of his age, concerned only with his ability to perform.

Most of them didn't even remember their mother. And nothing about fat, slovenly Inez gave them reason to respect or even to like the opposite sex. To the Maxfields, women were utilitarian like horses or mules. They saved a man the need to cook and tend the house. They relieved him periodically of his compelling male tensions.

At eleven, Inez's boy disappeared. Unconsciously Gabe's glance shifted from Mart to Les. Les had been with Rafael that day, and Gabe had never been entirely satisfied with his explanation that Rafael was seized by a hunting party of Comanches. But he hadn't probed. It simply didn't matter. Except that with Rafael gone, Inez left as well, and after that the Maxfield house was a house of men and they had to go to town, to the brothel on Prairie Street, when the need for a woman became too strong.

The face of that girl back there hung in Gabe's mind — her eyes . . . He turned his head and stared back.

Off to his right Mart yelled. Gabe reined his horse over and touched his spurs to its sides. As he rode over a slight rise, he heard

Les pounding up behind.

Mart was sitting his horse indolently beside the trail he had found. Without speaking, he moved out following it. Gabe rode beside him and Les fell in behind.

Thereafter they rode without speaking, each concerned with his own thoughts. And for the first time in his life, Gabe caught himself wondering what those thoughts might be.

Mart there. He was the softest of the lot, silent, taciturn. Mart was the best hand of the eight with horses, and the half dozen or so dogs the Maxfields kept adored him.

And Les. The dogs kept out of his way, slinking off to hide whenever he came near, or baring their teeth at him and raising the scruff of hair on the backs of their necks if he got within a dozen feet of them.

One thing, though. Comanches might raid other ranches — for horses, for scalps — but they never came near the Maxfield place. No one had ever dared challenge the Maxfield clan — not since all the boys were grown or partly grown, not until this stranger, Partin, came along.

Gabe's eyes narrowed slightly. His mouth thinned. They'd remedy that tomorrow.

He found his thoughts drifting back to the isolated ranch where he'd left his father and brothers. He found himself picking them out, one by one in his mind, and wondering at them.

Ezra. What had given Ezra his consuming passion for learning and books? What had made him work on his mother those last few years before she died, persuading her to take one of her rare stands against Miles and insist that he be allowed to go to town to school?

And once he had learned to read, what was it that had made Ezra's search for books so persistent and unending?

Not that his book learning hadn't been useful. It had accomplished things for the Maxfield clan that force could not. Right now, for instance, the fact that Ezra was Justice of the Peace would mean possession of the large Holcomb ranch.

And the girl for Alf. Gabe caught himself wondering what it would be like when Alf bedded her. A grin began at the corners of his mouth, suddenly fading as his eyes took on an angry look.

He shook himself visibly. Why shouldn't Alf have her? She was just a girl, like any girl. Too skinny to really interest a man. Too slight and weak to do much work. There were better ones than her back at the brothel in Comanche Wells.

The miles slid under him. Mart kept his horse between a trot and a slow lope, varying the gaits and occasionally dropping back to a walk. Gabe's thoughts went on, and he didn't like their turbulence. He'd get this over as soon as possible. He'd see that Partin was killed and would pack his body back to Comanche Wells so there wouldn't be any future repercussions about the sheriff's death.

Taking him back would mean that they'd have to hurry. He wouldn't keep long in this goddam heat.

The three rode on.

Luke Partin slept fitfully that night, tormented by recurring nightmares.

His last dream had been that the eight Maxfields were creeping up the slope. He saw them, saw their faces, and had known he had no chance. It was pure relief to wake and find that the land still lay empty before the cave, to find that it had only been a dream.

To be doomed, and to live again. It gave him strength. First he took a long, cool drink. And then he ate, ravenously now for the first time in several days.

Afterwards he stood in the shade of the bluff, staring out across the rolling, empty land. He wondered how many of them would come. Would all eight come, or would they leave some behind at the Holcomb ranch? He hoped they didn't, even though it would make the odds against him insurmountable. No telling what might happen to Nancy Holcomb if she were left for any length of time with a bunch of men like that.

Not that she deserved much better, as stubborn as she was. Yet Luke knew that if he had his roots as deep in a place as Nancy Holcomb had, he'd stay and fight and die, if need be, to keep it safe.

Out there, as far as the eye could see, a tiny dust cloud raised, and moved with the passing minutes almost imperceptibly towards him. Sometimes it disappeared, but it always reappeared, and it was always a little nearer each time it did.

Indians — or the Maxfields. Probably the latter, travelling along following trail. That was the route he and Nancy had followed coming here.

Luke scowled. He had seen a lot in his thirty-some-odd years. He had travelled a lot of miles but, he thought, wryly, he was exactly where he had been when he started, owning nothing, having no roots anywhere.

He'd been running all his life, he realized, towards something or away from something.

But running. And for what? Why? Right now he had no future and there was no place else to run.

He guessed that people were what their early lives made of them. Like Nancy Holcomb; loving a place and the memories it held enough to give her life for it. That was hard for Luke to understand. He'd never owned anything and neither had his father. He'd been raised on a rented farm where two-thirds of the crop went for rent and there was never enough left. His father worked himself and his children almost to death trying, but it was a game he couldn't win. He died and left them all without a thing.

Luke installed his mother and the younger kids in a shack in town and took a job, riding for the outfit of old Knute Finn west of the Colorado. He sent his money home, and after a few years found himself on the same treadmill his father had fought so many years.

Diphtheria took the kids, his brothers and sisters, and his mother married again. Luke drifted on.

Up and down the land. Mining silver on the sly in Mexico until the Rurales caught him at it and chased him across the border. Line-riding in Colorado, a hitch with the

Colorado Volunteers, and a wound at La Glorieta Pass, up in New Mexico. When that was healed, more riding, more drifting, competent enough at every thing he did, but suspicious of anything that would hold him still, put him into the trap his father had been in.

Now, this was the end of the long and aimless trail. And today, for the first time in his life, he saw what it was his father had found that had made it all worthwhile. Family ties. Sons to carry on when he was gone. Or one, at least, that lived.

The closest tie Luke had ever made had been with the Ortiz family. Only then Spence Maxfield had come along and killed them all.

The dust cloud was closer now, close enough so that by squinting and straining his eyes, he could occasionally make out the dark, tiny figures of horsemen through it and beneath it. He counted, squinting, but could never count any more than three.

And they weren't Indians. He could tell that by the way they rode. Two abreast, the other trailing along behind. White men rode abreast, but Indians never did.

He backed off from the rocks beside which he stood, aware that the sun had travelled over the top of the bluff and was beating down against his back with merciless intensity. He could feel the dampness of his shirt, the beads of sweat that had popped, in the last few minutes, from his forehead.

He lay down in the shade of the cave and closed his eyes. Wait. Wait for death to come. There was no way out. They had his trail and would follow it unerringly until they found him.

No use to make his way on foot to his horse. The animal was beat, as badly beat as Luke himself. They'd never outdistance that murderous three.

He lay as still as he could for almost an hour, trying to sleep, trying to rest. He'd need every bit of his strength before that sun went down. But if he did fight well, if he reduced the odds somewhat, then there *was* a chance. A chance to ride north in the darkness, with the Maxfields unable to follow until it was light again. And another stand, someplace else, if they caught up with him again.

Yes. It was possible for him to save himself. If he planned, and fought well, and made not a single mistake.

He got up at last and walked slowly into the sun. Its heat struck him like the blow of a fist and he could feel sweat spring from his pores at the impact of it.

He walked to the rocks and stared at the plain below. They came on at a slow lope, their heads bent as they studied the ground. He guessed that now they were no more than two or three miles away.

They split after a brief halt and a conference, following separate trails that Luke had made travelling to and from water. But they joined again where the trails picked their way out on top.

Luke knew what he had to do. He had to draw them here. He couldn't let them follow those trails out on top of the bluff, where they were certain to find his horse. If he did, he'd be out here afoot and even if he drove the Maxfields off, he'd have lost the fight.

He returned to the cave and picked up his rifle. He checked its loads. Then he went back out and found himself a narrow spot of shade behind a rock. He lay down, wriggled around until he was comfortable, then raised the rifle.

He sighted long and carefully on the leading horseman, calculating range, windage, the downhill drop of the bullet automatically in his mind. Holding slightly left, and about a foot above the man, he let his finger tighten almost imperceptibly against the trigger.

The rifle jumped, its roar thunderous in the complete stillness of this place.

He heard his bullet strike, but already knew where it had struck, for the sound was slow in reaching him. He saw the horse of the lead rider flinch as violently as he might shy from a rattlesnake in the trail. He saw the animal try to rear, barely clearing his front feet from the ground. He saw the horse go to his knees, then roll on to his side.

The man leaped clear, as did the others, and all three ran like rabbits for the cover of some rocks and brush.

In the echoing wake of Luke's shot, all was suddenly and completely still. The remaining two Maxfield horses had galloped off for a couple of hundred yards. Now they were cropping grass unconcernedly. The third horse kicked for several moments and then lay still.

Luke didn't move. He had spotted the places where each of the three had disappeared and kept his eyes on them. But nothing moved.

Minutes passed, dragging. The two horses moved into a draw and disappeared. The land seemed empty again, with only the body of the horse to say it was not.

Luke's mouth made a grim smile. The

Maxfields were competent at this. They had spotted Luke's location from that puff of smoke and knew he couldn't move without being seen. So they were content to wait, and not foolish enough to risk drawing Indians by a lot of pointless shooting. Probably two of them were trying to sleep right now, while the third kept watch.

But when the darkness came — when the light faded enough to allow them to move — then they'd be coming.

Chapter Nine

The daylight hours passed. Luke saw nothing whatever of the Maxfields — no movement of any kind. He heard nothing either.

The sun slipped behind the western horizon. From the thin scattering of clouds in the western sky, a brilliant orange reflected upon the land.

Still there was no movement down there in the rocks where the Maxfields were. Luke waited. Moving under cover of early darkness was a game that two could play. He wouldn't just wait up here for them to come.

Slowly, the clouds faded from orange to purple and at last to grey. Luke didn't stir. He stared down, waiting until the time when objects would no longer be distinguishable even at a hundred yards. Only then would he dare to move.

At last he got up and, with his back to the wall of the rim, eased carefully away from the overhang, moving slowly and smoothly, making no sudden or abrupt movements that might catch their eyes.

He knew they were coming, though he couldn't see and he couldn't hear. Playing a deadly game of stalking, they would hunt him as they might hunt a wounded lion capable of inflicting considerable punishment if he wasn't approached with care.

Fifty feet, a hundred, and still he moved away. Not until he was a full two hundred yards from the overhang did he stop.

As he had moved along, all light had faded completely from the sky. The stars winked out.

Luke stopped, his knuckles white against the stock of his rifle. He strained his ears, listening. He heard a rock grate against another down there on the slope, and nothing else.

Even had his ears not told him they were coming and his brain not known they were there, another sense would have told him — a purely animal sense that seldom came into play. Perhaps it was awakened by the menace of their thoughts, by their virulence. But it was working now, and it made the hairs on his neck stir.

Motionless he stood, and he might have been a part of the rock wall, warm from the afternoon sun, against his back. Another rock broke loose down there on the slope and rolled away from whomever had stirred it, to crash against another, bigger rock where the slope levelled into the plain.

A cool breeze blew now along the rim, chilling his body beneath his sweat-soaked shirt. Or maybe the chill came from something else — from knowing they were stalking him and would kill instantly and without hesitation if they encountered him.

Straining his ears, he waited and tried to guess how they would come. One from below, he supposed, another from each side along the foot of the rim. Which ever one approached from this direction should be coming along here soon.

His ears picked up a sound, one he did not immediately identify. He turned his head and, instinctively, his rifle barrel towards it.

He saw a movement a dozen yards away — a vague, shadowy movement, and heard the sound again. Clothing, brushing lightly against the face of rock, and an accompanying, softer sound, that of crushed rock and dirt compressing beneath a carefully placed foot when weight comes slowly down upon it.

He started violently, as tense as he was, when a night bird made its eerie scream atop the rim. And brought his gun up to a ready position.

Starting like that, he must have made a sound. Those before him ceased.

Waiting again, scarcely daring to breathe. Had he misjudged their ability as hunters? Had he given himself too much credit? What if they'd seen him leave the overhang, and were even now approaching from the front, from the downhill side, and from behind?

Inwardly he shrugged. If they were that sly, he was dead anyway. But he didn't think they were.

The sound again — now less than a dozen yards away. The waiting became intolerable. Every nerve in him screamed for action, for something to break this deadly inactivity.

Shadowy movement again, startling because it was so close. And then, as the breeze stilled or shifted, a smell of rank, unwashed clothing, stale with sweat, rancid with grease and campfire smoke. The smell of stale tobacco, and the leathery, sweaty smell of boots.

Luke could face a man with a gun in his hand in broad daylight and feel no fear, no dread. But to face a man in the dark, knowing there were others, without knowing which of them you faced . . .

He drove the barrel of the rifle forward,

felt it encounter the yielding body of the man in front of him. He heard the explosive grunt it drew from the startled man. He saw the man double slightly from the excruciating pain of its hard-driving tiny muzzle sinking itself into his belly.

And he tried to club the rifle.

Instantly he wished he had simply pulled the trigger and killed the man, but he'd been trying to avoid the noise, knowing it would draw the others at a run.

The shadowy man moved with the speed of a striking snake, unslowed by the pain of the savage jab he had received from Luke's gun. He drove forward, his shoulder striking Luke and knocking him viciously back against the wall.

Luke's head slammed against the unyielding rock with a crack. His senses reeled. The impact brought immediate pain to his wounds and the feel of wet, fresh blood.

Hands groped for him and he raised a knee, knowing it struck a vital spot by the grunt of pain that escaped his adversary's lips. Again he tried to club the gun, but failed when it hit the wall behind his back.

He released it instantly. Too late now to worry about noise. The sounds of their struggle must have carried a quarter mile with this sheer rim to act as a sounding board. Even now the others must be racing here.

He whipped his body with every bit of strength he possessed and flung the other man off and away, for several feet. He didn't try to come to his feet, but clawed out his revolver while still on his knees.

Centring instinctively on the moving, scrambling shape before him, he pulled the trigger and thumbed the hammer back again.

But the other had stopped, and put both hands down upon the rocky ground to steady himself. Luke could hear his breath, rasping and harsh and difficult, gustily blowing in and out of his heaving lungs.

He froze, listening, the gun still centred on that immobilized figure before him. A scrambling a hundred yards down the slope told him someone was clawing up that way. Rocks kicked up along the rim a little farther off told him the third man was racing toward him from that direction. The two would come together a little to his right, and if this business wasn't finished then . . .

He said harshly, "Which one are you?"

No answer. He said, "You son-of-a-bitch, do you want your guts blown out?"

A moment's silence, and then a pain-filled, choking voice, "I'm Mart."

"Who are the others?"

"Gabe and Les. And they'll get you, you bastard. They'll kill you slow like the Indians do."

"Maybe. Where's the rest of you?"

No answer. Luke released the hammer slowly with his thumb, then cocked it again audibly. A sullen answer, "Back at the Holcomb place."

"The girl with them?"

"Yeah."

"She been hurt?" He wondered at the anxiety with which he awaited the answer to that.

"Why should they hurt her? She's goin' to marry Alf."

The scrambling on the slope was closer now, and the breathing of the man who made the noise was audible even over the crashing sounds of rocks below him. He called hoarsely and breathlessly, "Mart? What's goin' on? You all right?"

Luke whispered savagely, "You yell and I'll blow your brains out!"

Mart remained silent. His words of a few moments before kept churning in Luke Partin's brain, and all they churned up was anger, cold and implacable and savage. Nancy Holcomb would not, he knew, ever have agreed to marry one of this filthy bunch unless she were forced to do so. And the methods that must have been used to force her consent could only have been as ugly as the men who thought them up.

He whispered, "How the hell can you make her marry Alf? All she has to do is refuse when she gets in front of the preacher."

The wounded man chuckled painfully. "Not if the preacher's a Justice of the Peace. Not if he's Ezra Maxfield."

His last words ended with a weak and pain-filled groan. Luke eased to his feet, watchful for sudden movement from Mart, listening intently both to Mart's harsh breathing and the rapidly approaching sounds. "Who's coming up the slope?"

He got no answer, and swung his head. He could hear nothing from Mart now. And Mart was down, flat on the ground, curled up like a child asleep.

He'd get no more from Mart. The man was either dead or unconscious and from Luke's standpoint it didn't matter which. He was out of the fight — no longer a threat. The odds were two to one right now, and if he could even them a little more . . .

Luke eased away cautiously, sacrificing speed for silence. If they didn't know where he was, they'd move with a hell of a lot more care than they would if they could spot his location.

He heard their surprised exclamations when they discovered Mart. He saw the flare of a sulphur match, saw them kneeling beside Mart's body.

He raised his gun, suddenly aware that he had left his rifle back there where it had fallen. He thumbed back the hammer and tightened his finger on the trigger.

But he never squeezed it. The match went out, eliminating all certainty from his target.

Their voices were low, their words indistinguishable. The tones of them were not. It took no perception to detect their fury. Luke was rapidly becoming a scourge to the Maxfield clan. He had killed Spence, and now he had probably killed Mart too. They'd hunt him down if it took a year. They'd hunt him down even if the hunt carried them half-way across the continent.

Their talking stopped, and all sound ceased. Luke stooped and took off his boots. He unbuttoned his shirt and stuffed them inside, one on each side. He'd cut his feet to ribbons and probably fill them with cactus spines, but maybe silence would keep him alive.

He could move faster now, and make less sound. His ears, not bothered by sounds he made himself, could hear the Maxfields better as they came along behind.

He walked a quarter mile. Sharp rocks cut his feet, and once he stepped squarely upon a prickly pear. It took all his will to keep from grunting with the pain, took all his will to continue walking on the spine-laden foot.

But on he went. Where the trail went up, he'd make a stand. Given the advantage of height, he'd take a chance on facing them.

On and on. The distance from the overhang to the trail he had used to go out on top seemed doubled. But at last he saw it, nearly having passed it in the pitch darkness.

Carefully, so as not to loosen any rocks, he climbed up for a dozen yards. And squatted down behind a rock to wait.

CHAPTER TEN

There was a time, as he waited there, when bleak hopelessness came over him. Weakness made his head swim, made his vision blur. The bandages Nancy Holcomb had put upon his wounds were soaked again, and he could ill afford to lose that blood. If it came to hand-to-hand combat with the Maxfields now, he knew he would certainly lose.

The minutes dragged. The Maxfields were, he guessed, coming on with considerably more caution than they had before. Mart's death had sobered them, destroyed their arrogant sense of invincibility.

He strained his ears, scarcely daring to breathe. It was a temptation to retreat on up the trail, get his horse and ride away. But he knew such a course would be shortsighted. He had to stop them, once and for all. He had to even the odds or they'd overtake him tomorrow sometime and then he wouldn't have a chance.

So he waited and listened, breathing slowly and almost silently through his open mouth.

His nerves drew tight. His hands trembled ever so slightly. His eyes were narrowed to mere slits, trying to pierce the darkness of the night.

Comanches could not have approached more silently. But at last his straining eyes caught the merest blur of movement.

He knew his course. He'd have to fire and instantly change position. He'd have to draw their fire, else he'd have no sure target at which he could shoot. If they went on past, then this game of cat-and-mouse would be repeated again tonight. And his tight-drawn nerves had already taken all they could.

He raised his gun. The hammer was back, so he didn't need to cock it. He had three shots and that was all. There'd be no time for reloading.

Waste one shot to draw their fire. And two would be left. Two shots to put at least one of them permanently out of the fight. If he used them both unsuccessfully he'd be defenceless and vulnerable and would then have no choice but flight.

Another vague and shadowy movement. Luke fired.

He heard no cry of pain, heard no body fall. But he heard their grunts of surprise even as he moved.

Violently, with no thought of his wounds, he sprang up and darted to one side, careless of footing, knowing only that their bullets would, in half a second, be probing the spot where he had been.

The two gun flashes came almost as one, no more than thirty feet away. And Luke, crouched and ready, fired without hesitation, without thought, first at one gun flash and then the other.

He wasted not a second's time. With an empty gun, he was finished. Crouching low, running, he went up the rocky trail.

Bullets followed his course, ricocheting from nearby rocks with savage whines and sailing off to strike again elsewhere. Gun flashes bloomed below him, but he didn't turn to look.

At last he could run no more. Breath whistled in and out of his starving lungs. His muscles were like water, his legs and arms incredibly heavy.

He collapsed to the steep trail, bracing his feet so that he couldn't slide. Panting harshly and raggedly, he stared down towards the foot of the rim.

The gun flashes continued, probing

blindly now that there was no sound to guide their aim. Flashes from but a single gun, he saw with vast relief. Then one of his shots had scored.

Below him, whichever one of the two was shooting apparently emptied his gun, for the shooting stopped abruptly. He heard a low, continuous groaning, and a voice that carried well in the still air. "Les! Where you hit?"

"Right in the ass. Goddam that son-of-a-bitch! Go get him, Gabe!"

"You bleedin' much?"

Another groan, but no answer. Then at last the wounded man's outraged voice, "If you laugh, I'll kill you! Go on, get out of here! Get him before he gets away!"

"He'll keep. I ain't goin' to leave you here, an' Mart's got to be buried. We'll get him, though, don't worry about that. We'll get him if it takes a thousand years."

A long, slow sigh escaped Luke's lips. He had bought the time he had to have. Gabe Maxfield was going to return to the Holcomb place with Mart's body and with Les. That would take all night at least. It would take all of tomorrow for them to return to this spot and pick up his trail again . . . It added up to a twenty-four hour start on them. It added up to a chance to live, if he wasn't too weak to travel, if all that bleeding hadn't stolen too damn much of his strength.

He turned and carefully began to climb again, silently so as not to attract their notice, slowly because that was the only way he could go.

Down below he could still hear them, grunting, cursing, as Gabe doctored Les's wound, then helped him to his feet and down the slope to where their horses had been left.

Resting at the top of the rim, he heard the sounds of their voices gradually fade and die. Later, he heard Gabe grunting heavily as he climbed the slope after Mart's body. He didn't move, for he knew that now, for a while, he had better be still and give his bleeding wounds a chance to clot.

Gabe half carried, half dragged Mart's body down the slope. Luke heard him fall several times, and each time he shouted with profane wrath. Gabe had probably not, in his whole life, been so furiously angry and so helpless to do something about it. Luke grinned wryly.

Not that it was funny. It wasn't. There were five more able-bodied Maxfields back at the Holcomb place. They'd all come after Luke, leaving Les behind to guard the girl.

If the Comanches came while the others were away . . .

Luke closed his mind to thoughts of that. If Comanches came to the Holcomb place — well, he certainly couldn't stop them. Even if he were there, he'd be little help. Nancy had made her choice and would now have to take her chances.

He heard the hoofbeats of the Maxfields' two horses fade away into nothingness, heading south. He walked back to where his own horse was picketed, and there, in a small ravine, built a fire. It was a risk, he knew, but he couldn't travel with his foot full of cactus spines.

It took him almost half an hour to pull them out, and at that he didn't get them all. Then he reloaded his gun. When he had finished, he pulled on his boots, killed the fire, saddled up and mounted. He rode out, heading north.

He had covered less than a mile before he stopped. The horse, still not completely recovered from the hard use Luke had given him over the past few weeks, was content to stand, head hanging.

Luke's head was light, but his body felt heavy. He had overestimated his strength. He still was not ready to face the hostile country ahead. He had to have more time.

But how to buy it? He had bought twenty-four hours back there at the foot of the rim. If he had three times that long he might be able to rest himself enough. He might be able to put sufficient distance between himself and this place so that the Maxfields would never catch up with him.

He frowned, staring down at his horse's hanging head. There was a way, all right, but it involved considerable risk to himself. With the time he had wasted pulling cactus spines, he might not be able to manage it at all.

But he could try.

He reined around suddenly, touched spurs to his horse's sides and forced the animal into a brisk, fast trot. He headed south.

Blind in the darkness, he was forced to travel almost exclusively by instinct. Only the fact that the Maxfields were handicapped by a dead man and a wounded one, and by their loss of one of their horses, gave him hope that he could pull it off.

He rode for the better part of an hour, alternating his horse's gait between that fast trot and a rocking lope. He could miss them a mile in the darkness, but he didn't think he would. They were a vocal bunch. Les would be groaning and cursing almost continually, and Gabe would be trying to shut him up.

At intervals, Luke stopped, holding his horse then utterly still while he strained his ears ahead. And at last, off to his right quarter, he heard them, shouting at each other with baulked fury.

Luke made mental note of the bearing of the sounds. Then he spurred his horse ahead.

He rode for another fifteen minutes and stopped a second time. Again he listened intently and took a bearing on the sounds.

And on he went. The third time he stopped he was well ahead of them.

He dismounted here and tied his horse to a clump of brush. He walked painfully from that place to the top of a low point and listened intently again.

Fainter now, but still bickering, still wrangling. He grinned to himself, wondering how Les was sitting his saddle and wishing he could see. He was willing to bet that Les was travelling belly-down across his saddle like a sack of grain. He was willing to bet that Les was as maddened, as filled with helpless fury as a rattler prodded and tormented beyond his endurance.

He listened for five minutes, then quickly altered his position by a couple of hundred yards. He listened another two or three minutes, and altered his position again. This time he found a ravine into which he could climb and from there look up at the place he estimated they had to pass, silhouetted against the stars.

Nervously he thumbed back the hammer of his gun, and wished he had his rifle back. If he pulled this off, there'd be time to return and pick it up.

Slowly they came on. He couldn't see them yet, but he could hear them plain enough. Apparently they were so angry that they didn't even care if they ran into a party of Comanches. Probably they'd welcome it, for it would give them a chance to work off some of their murderous rage.

Luke grinned slightly again. If they were furious now, how would they be ten minutes from now? His grin faded. His muscles tensed intolerably. He waited impatiently for the seemingly endless minutes to pass.

Chapter Eleven

Gabe had ridden for an hour, his thoughts seething, his anger maintaining a steady heat. To be going away from Partin when more than anything in the world he wanted to be going towards him — that was what hurt.

He had no feeling of uneasiness. No premonition of danger touched him. His horse's ears pricked, and then lay back, but Gabe was so occupied with his own bitter thoughts that he didn't notice.

But when the horse nickered, to be answered by another nicker off there to the right, that woke Gabe to the present with a shock, with a sinking feeling of disaster.

Once more he had been a fool — he knew that before any shots rang out, before any gun flares lighted the darkness in front of him. Brooding on his baulked fury, he had let Partin outguess him again.

His thoughts were like lightning that first

moment. He realized immediately that had he thought about it he would have expected exactly this from Partin. The man had gained thirty-six hours for himself by killing Mart and wounding Les. He could gain another thirty-six by killing a couple of horses, or by killing Gabe.

Almost as these thoughts touched him, Gabe was on the move. He flung himself from his horse in a single, smooth movement, and hit the ground rolling. Scarcely had he cleared the horse's back when he saw, not a dozen yards away, the flare of Partin's gun, once, twice, and heard the reports hard upon the heels of the flashes.

And another sound, that of bullets striking flesh. Gabe's horse reared, nickered shrilly, and fell over backwards with a ground-shaking crash. The horse bearing the wounded Les made no sound at all. He just seemed to stumble and then collapsed upon the ground.

Only Les's horse wasn't dead. Down on the ground, with Les's legs pinned beneath him, he thrashed and kicked violently.

Gabe gave no thought to Les. Let him extricate himself. Right now all he could think was that Partin was less than a hundred yards away.

He scrambled to his feet, running towards

Partin the instant he gained them. He snatched his revolver from its holster.

Recklessly, with complete disregard for his own safety, he charged towards the place Partin had been. He stumbled and fell headlong, his face skidding in the dirt. Spitting mud and dry dirt, he clawed again to his feet, nearly out of his mind with rage.

But now he stopped, and listened, and heard Partin's running feet as he went towards the place he had left his horse.

Now Gabe had a direction, and he ran again, knowing all Partin had to do to win this third round was to mount and ride away.

His breath whistled in and out of his lungs. Behind him he could hear Les yelling and the horse still thrashing. He ran on, and at last he saw the moving bulk of a horse in the darkness before him.

He flung up his gun, hammer back, and fired two shots rapidly at the moving shape, but he didn't stop.

Ahead, the slap of a man hitting the saddle, the jingle of spurs, the flapping of stirrup leathers against a horse's sides. And the bulk diminished, accompanied by the rapid pound of hoofs.

And now Gabe stopped, knowing with nearly intolerable fury that again he had miscalculated. If he had hauled to a stop the instant he saw the horse . . . If he'd sighted and fired carefully . . .

But he hadn't, and now Partin was gone.

Raging, Gabe emptied his gun in the direction Partin had disappeared. And then he stood, breathing hard, both from anger and his run, trembling from head to foot.

Killing Partin had, at first, been only a necessary thing, a thing undertaken more out of a realization that this challenger of the clan had to die to discourage others than from any real hatred or desire to get even. There was not enough affection between members of the Maxfield clan to arouse such a burning need for vengeance, and Gabe had never gotten along very well with Spence anyway.

Now, however, Partin's challenge had become an intensely personal thing. Hatred, frustration and fury ate away at Gabe's brain. His trembling increased. He shook his fist at the heavens and screamed curses at the skies. His voice roared across the vastness of this empty land, like the ravings of one demented.

And then, at last, he collapsed upon the ground, still shaking but weak and spent.

In Gabe's mind now there was nothing important, nothing worthwhile except the pursuit and death of Luke Partin. He would pursue that end henceforth, until he was dead or until Luke was dead. If it took him all the rest of his life. If he sacrificed every one of his brothers and himself as well.

He got to his feet and staggered back towards the horses. Les's animal was still thrashing. Gabe started fumbling with his gun in the darkness, trying to reload. He spilled powder on the ground — more than he got into the gun. Cursing savagely, he finally finished, but by that time he had changed his mind about shooting the horse. Hurt or not, goddam it, that horse was going to pack Les and Mart back to the Holcomb place.

He holstered the gun and walked over to the horse. He pulled Les out from beneath it with cruel disregard for Les's pain. Then he began kicking the horse, savagely, expertly.

The animal struggled violently and finally heaved himself to his feet. He stood trembling, carrying a front leg clear of the ground.

Gabe struck a match and knelt to look. Luke's bullet had shattered the horse's left front leg just below the knee. But it wasn't bleeding much.

Cursing softly at the darkness, Gabe went

to the other horse and took Mart's body from it. He hoisted the body to the back of the wounded horse. Then he helped Les to his feet and eased him up, face down, across the saddle. He tied both Mart and Les to the saddle in much the same way he'd tie down a deer.

Then, carrying his rifle in one hand and holding the horse's reins in the other, he began to walk south towards the Holcomb place.

And as he walked, he planned what he would do to Luke when he finally caught up with him. There were things the Indians did to a captive, and Gabe knew them all for he had seen, in his years in Comanche-land, the human wreckage the Comanches sometimes left behind.

Luke would die slowly, and that Holcomb girl, for letting him get away and helping him, would watch him die.

Endlessly Gabe walked, dragging the hobbling horse behind. The bright edge of his fury dulled, for it could not sustain itself at the pitch Luke Partin had roused it to.

But an ugliness remained, a crawling savagery that did not go away. With every mile, with every aching step, hatred for Luke became more of an obsession with Gabe until he could think of nothing else, until he wanted to think of nothing else.

Gabe began to hate his brother Les because Les slowed him down and delayed the time when he could resume the pursuit of Luke. He hated the horse because it limped and pulled against the reins. He hated Mart, even though Mart was dead, because Mart added to the weight the horse must carry and so added to the delay.

Dawn came, but Gabe would not stop and rest. Les cried out with pain and thirst, and begged for a drink, but Gabe savagely put him off.

He plodded along as the sun came up. He plodded along, his face grim, his mouth set, his eyes narrowed and hard as the sun raised in the sky and beat fiercely upon the plain.

All through the day he continued, and Les only got a drink on the few occasions when they crossed a stream, at which time Gabe drank too.

His boot soles wore through and he was forced to stop and pack layers of cloth from his pants legs in them. His legs were like lead and he staggered now. But he wouldn't slow and he wouldn't stop. On and on he went like a man in a dream.

Night again, and dawn, and at sunup he walked into the yard at the Holcomb place, nearly dead from exhaustion but with the burning light in his narrowed eyes undiminished, undimmed.

He collapsed a hundred yards from the house. His brothers came out and carried him inside.

CHAPTER TWELVE

After Gabe left with Mart and Les, Nancy went about preparing supper for the rest without being told. For one thing, she knew it would help her shattered nerves to keep busy. For another, she knew that well-fed men are more agreeable than hungry ones. If she gave them no reason to suspect that she intended to try and get away, it might be easier to do so when the right time came.

She found, to her surprise, that there was an unknown reservoir of strength in her, a thing that enabled her to quiet the squirrel-cage racing of her trapped mind, that enabled her to plan. They had threatened her with every terrible thing possible; she had lived with the threats, with the certainty that at least part of them would be carried out. Now, instead of shivering in abject fear of them, she'd do something. Even if it failed. At least, if and when those awful things they had promised happened to her, she would know she had tried, and had done something, and had fought back.

Sitting around the table wolfing their food, they were more like hogs at a trough than men at a table. They ate, to a large extent, with their fingers. She repressed a shudder and instead studied them, one after the other.

Miles, the father, sat at the head of the long, rough-hewn table, greying and bushy-haired. She could tell, looking at him, that he took a perverse pride in the brutality, in the coarseness of his sons. And yet, she had noticed one thing about Miles. When he first sat down, he had picked up the table-ware and begun to use it unthinkingly. There were other things about him too. He had known a better life — somewhere, sometime — but it was almost as though he had chosen to deliberately scorn it, as though he were wallowing in the bestiality to which he and his sons had descended.

Catching himself using the tableware she had provided, catching himself reaching for the napkin beside his plate, he had, in sudden fury, swept the whole place setting before him to the floor, breaking most of the dishes and making Nancy jump with startled fright. "Never mind all this goddam foofaraw! Just give us the food!" Then he looked down the table, grinning with malicious pride. "Damn 'em, I wish they could see their precious grandsons now."

Alf looked at him bemusedly. "Who, Pa? What are you talkin' about?"

"Your mother's folks. Said I wasn't good enough. Said I was trash. I just wish they could see the trash their daughter bore."

Alf said, "We ain't trash, Pa, an' it ain't right for you to say we are."

Ezra broke in, "Shut up, Alf, and eat."

Alf looked from Ezra to his father. He looked up at Nancy and grinned tentatively. He was utterly repulsive to her, and yet she did not miss the hint of shy wistfulness in his eyes.

He was, perhaps, more dangerous than all the rest to her, she thought. He was the baby of the family, the perpetual butt of their jokes. And while he might want to treat her decently, he would be driven by the need to prove himself by treating her in a way his brothers would both understand and approve. Nancy had become Alf's special problem, and the more he failed with her the more his brothers would taunt him, until he was driven to the kind of savage brutality they would approve.

And Ezra. A dried-up, middle-aged man whose ambition was boundless. He hated

137

his brothers; Nancy could see that in his eyes. But he knew he needed them. She could see something else in him, a kind of hunger as he looked up and down the table, at the way she had set it, at the way his brothers were eating. He touched the tableware tentatively, almost gingerly, plainly wanting to use it but too self-conscious to try.

Ezra was the lawyer, the Justice of the Peace. To be either, he had to have educated himself, but she supposed books had bean all he'd had. Now he was probably realizing he needed something more if he were to go on ahead. Some of the social graces so that he could mingle with people and not be scorned.

Ezra had the education. Nancy and this ranch would provide money. But to go where Ezra intended to go, he needed more, and for some reason he was realizing it tonight.

Her glance went on down the table. Vic sat across from Ezra on the old man's left. Vic's face was vacant, almost bovine. He had paid no attention at all to the conversation, probably had not even heard it. Vic was bigger, even, than Alf, but if he had any thoughts in his big, shaggy head, they didn't show in his face.

And Will, the fifth of those seated there. Will's eyes were quiet, thoughtful, and very sharp. Will hadn't said three words in all the time he'd been here, but Nancy had the feeling he hadn't missed a thing.

A forlorn hope touched her and went away. Perhaps they could be played against each other, but she doubted if she could manage it. She knew too little about them. All her knowledge of them must come from observation. No, her best chance lay in escape.

When they had finished eating, she picked up a bucket and started to go outside for water. Alf got up to follow, but Will said, "Let 'er go, Alf."

"Hell, she might get away."

"Where to? What's the matter, Alf, don't you reckon she's anxious to get back to you?"

Alf flushed and muttered something. Nancy glanced at Will gratefully. It was the first consideration shown her. She had been worrying about this — about not having any privacy at all.

She went outside. It wouldn't be smart to seize this first opportunity to escape. If she wasn't back within a reasonable length of time, they'd come after her.

The air outside was clean and fresh after

the reek of the house with so many un-washed men inside. She stood briefly in the middle of the yard, breathing it. Then she hurried towards the well.

Later, when they were all asleep . . . If she could slip out then, she'd have several hours in which to put distance between herself and here.

Returning to the house, she found herself dreading the coming night, wanting desperately to escape and yet fearing that almost as much as she feared staying here. She knew there was not much chance that she'd get away — less that she could safely reach a settlement someplace before they tracked her down.

She thought about Luke Partin. Why had she left him? It would have been better to stay with him and die with him than to be here alone with the Maxfield clan.

She wondered how he was faring, if he had enough to eat and drink, if his wounds were healing right. Tomorrow he'd have to face Gabe and Les and Mart. And he had even less chance of coming through alive than Nancy had to escape.

She could see in her mind the place she had left him, the overhang high under that rocky rim. She knew he would fight, and fight well too. If she could only reach him before the Maxfields did . . .

She went into the house, ignoring so far as possible the men inside. It angered her to see them here, lounging in the chairs her father and brother had used.

She stifled her anger and put water on the stove. She stoked the fire, and while the water heated, began to pick up the dishes preparatory to washing them.

Later, they assigned her the room she was used to sleeping in, and they themselves bedded down in the other room. They put no guard on her, probably counting on their own alertness, even in sleep, to prevent her trying to escape.

She closed the door and for a moment leaned against it weakly. She didn't know if she would have the necessary strength — to stay awake, to slip out through that room of snoring men into the outside air. Or the strength to ride away and keep going, no matter what.

She braced a chair against the door and bolted it — not with the hope of keeping them out if they chose to come in, but only so that she would be warned. Then she blew out the lamp and lay down, fully clothed.

How to mark the passage of time, when anxiety reached an almost intolerable pitch? She had intended letting tonight pass without making an attempt to escape. She had thought doing so would put them off guard.

But now, lying here tensely in the darkness, she knew she could not pretend with the Maxfield bunch. Nor could she stay another day without completely falling apart.

Escape through the window was out of the question, she knew. Her father had built the windows purposely narrow, to prevent the entrance of an Indian should the house be attacked by them. The window, while high enough, was less than five inches wide.

Occasionally she moved on the bed, so that if any of them were still awake they would hear it creak. The minutes dragged.

Deliberately she waited much longer than she thought necessary, knowing she was certain to think more time had passed than really had. But at last, when she was certain it was well past midnight, she got to her feet and went silently to the door, her shoes carried in one hand.

Carefully, making not the smallest sound, she removed the chair she had set against the knob, and slipped the bolt. She swung the door open as far as it would swing before it began to squeak. She stood there listening to their snores for a moment, repressing a shiver, and then stepped through.

Her eyes were used to the dark, and she knew the location of each piece of furniture in the room from memory. She threaded her way quickly and lightly between the sleeping forms on the floor. Once, as she was passing near one he rolled towards her, flinging out an arm. The hand brushed the hem of her skirt, and she gasped faintly. But the man didn't stir, and after a moment she went on again.

Across to the door, beginning to tremble now. She unbarred it and, so that it wouldn't squeak, lifted up on it as she swung it slowly open enough to allow her to slip on through.

And then outside, into the blessedly clear, clean air. There was no longer any hesitation in her. She ran across the yard, holding her skirts up so that she wouldn't trip on them. Straight to the corral, and in through the gate as soon as she had it unbarred.

There were a dozen or so horses in the corral, the Maxfields having run in a bunch of her father's horses. But even in the darkness she was able to recognize, by the shape of his head and body, one she had ridden before and knew was easy to catch. She fumbled along the corral fence until she found a piece of rope, then went to the horse and slipped it around his neck.

The others milled, galloping back and forth. The racket they made put her into a near frenzy of fear, but there was nothing she could do about it. They weren't used to women near them, and the more she tried to quiet them, the more terrified they became.

She led the hammerheaded grey she had caught to the gate and out through it. Saddles and bridles were piled carelessly beside the gate against the fence. She didn't try to find her own but went to the nearest one and, after bridling the horse and throwing on a stiff, odorous saddle blanket, flung up the saddle and cinched it down.

With a final glance towards the house, she swung astride. No time or opportunity to take a canteen full of water, or any food. No time for anything save just getting away. She reined around and headed north.

Out of the darkness before her came a low chuckle, one that made her start violently. Someone stepped from the shadows and seized the headstall of her horse.

The horse didn't shy, indicating he had known the man was there all the time. If only she had known as well!

It was Will, the quiet, watchful one. Nancy said, "Let me go! Please!"

Again that humourless chuckle. "Get

down, missy. You ain't goin' nowhere. What's the matter with you, don't you like our company? Alf won't like hearin' that. He was thinkin' you was gettin' kind of fond of him."

Suddenly all she had endured from these men became too much for her. Blindly she slashed at him with the ends of her reins.

They caught him across the face with a sharp, loud slap. He lunged back, but he did not let go of the horse's headstall. The animal tried to rear, but Will held on, dragging him down by sheer strength and weight.

And then Will was beside her. He seized her arm and yanked her headlong from the saddle. She hit the ground with a thump that shook her teeth.

Releasing the horse, he yanked her up. He slapped her face, hard, first on the left side, then backhanded on the right. "You little bitch! Get back in that house!"

Nancy could feel tears of helplessness and hopelessness welling up into her eyes. She could feel her body beginning to shake.

She fought both furiously. Abuse her they might, but they wouldn't make her cry. They wouldn't!

She thought of her father and Ben. They hadn't raised her to cope with things like this. But they had both been strong, quiet men with reserves of strength that enabled them to deal with whatever came along.

And Nancy would be the same. She wouldn't break down and she wouldn't quit! Somehow she'd get hold of a weapon and hide it, if it was only a kitchen knife. And the first one that touched her would get a whole lot more than he bargained for.

They might kill her, but there were worse things than that. With a show of meekness, Nancy trudged away towards the house.

Chapter Thirteen

A dozen yards from the house, Will yelled, and by the time Nancy reached the door, a lamp was on. Will kicked open the door and shoved her in. He said, "I don't think she wants to marry you, Alf. She was tryin' to run away."

The other four were up, tousled and untidy from sleep. Alf and Ezra were in their underwear, long, red-flannel underwear that was dirty and stained with sweat. It bagged both at the seat and at the knees, making them look slightly ridiculous. But Nancy didn't smile. She just hated them, virulently and silently with her eyes.

Vic and Miles had apparently slept in their pants, removing only their shirts. Miles growled, "I told you she'd try it."

"Then why didn't you stay awake an' watch?"

Miles glared. "Don't you use that tone on me!"

Will didn't reply. He only chuckled. "Maybe you'd better go in an' get in bed with her, Alf. That way, you'll know if she tries to get away. Hell, you're goin' to marry her anyhow. It wouldn't hurt to jump the gun. Gabe said you was to court her, an' what better place than snug in bed?"

Alf flushed painfully. He glanced at Nancy, then down at his feet. Noticing that he was in his underwear, he snatched for his pants, turned his back and started to put them on. With one leg in and the other part way in, he lost his balance and fell, and his brothers roared.

Alf got up, his face sweating and painfully red. But there was something in his eyes Nancy hadn't seen there before. Anger. Raw, unthinking fury. Perhaps he had stood their ridicule before, but now it was different. Now their ridicule was hurting because it was making him look a fool in Nancy's eyes and apparently he desperately wanted anything but that.

Angry as she was, she suddenly had a strange compulsion to laugh. Alf Maxfield was in love with her.

Will gestured towards her room with his head. "Get on in there. An' put your mind on what Gabe said you'd get if you tried to run away."

A quirting. Nancy knew. She also knew that Gabe would do it, or have it done. In front of the whole, dirty, Maxfield clan. Unless Alf . . .

She crossed the room, avoiding them nervously as she went. Alf might be used, but Nancy couldn't do it. She couldn't play up to Alf if her life depended on it — as well it might.

But she did feel a grain of hope. The fury in Alf's eyes was the first crack in the Maxfields' solidarity that had appeared up to now. And it might be used, to split them wider apart.

Behind her, she heard Will's voice, holding authority in Gabe's absence: "Go on in the room with her, Alf. What you do to her is your own damn business but see she don't get out again."

Vic chuckled almost like a demented child. "Can we watch 'im, Will?"

Will said drily, "Probably nothin' to watch — if I know Alf."

Again the whole clan roared.

Once inside the room, Nancy turned. That raw fury was in Alf's eyes again. His face was mottled, sweating still. The muscles along his boil-covered jaws were tight; his mouth was compressed.

Dirty he might be, pimpled and unsure.

But he was dangerous, and the more they taunted him the more dangerous he would become.

She knew, as surely as she had ever known anything, that Alf would try to prove himself with her before the night was out. And if she couldn't talk him out of it, if she fought him and made him look a fool . . . Well, it would be Alf that wielded the quirt when Gabe returned. Furious already at his brothers for their ridicule, his fury would turn itself on her if she caused them to ridicule him further.

She turned her back on Alf, wincing as she heard the door close, as she heard the instantaneous roar of laughter from the other side of it.

"I'm awfully tired," she said timidly.

It was the worst thing she could have said, because he took it for an invitation. He licked his heavy lips, shifted his eyes back and forth between Nancy and the bed. Then he took a step towards her, an odd, scared look coming into his eyes, the flush going out of his face.

She backed away. She could imagine the laughter that would follow any sound she made. She backed slowly towards the far corner of the room. She said, "Please . . . don't. Tell them anything you want, but please . . ."

His eyes were hot now. He licked his lips again. His hands came up, ready to seize her. She saw that they were dirty and covered with grease from supper.

She shuddered visibly. That stopped him for an instant, but only for an instant. Then he came on, his eyes still hot, but ugly now.

Words came whispering from between his lips. "I ain't that bad, by God. I ain't that bad. Plenty of women have liked me. Plenty of women. An' by God, you will too, once I've showed you a thing or two."

She darted out of the corner and felt his hand touch her bare arm. She darted to another corner, the one diagonally across the room, rubbing the place on her arm where his hand had touched.

She felt trapped, frantic. She felt that if he seized her, if he got her in his arms, she'd lose her mind completely. She'd become a demented, vacant-eyed thing like a woman she had once seen who had been recaptured from Comanches. She'd heard her father say that the poor soul's mind had taken refuge in insanity, being unable to live with the awful things that had happened to her.

Nancy herself would be like that, she knew, if Alf did what he intended to do to her.

His eyes were angry now. He came across the room as though trying to catch a bird, cautiously and moving with infinite care. Like a boy, angered at a bird he cannot catch, determined to hurt it in return once he did succeed in catching it.

And suddenly, trapped in that room with Alf, Nancy's whole outlook changed. Anger flowed through her veins, heating her blood. Her face turned pale with it, and her eyes sparkled dangerously. She said furiously, "Damn you, if you put just one of those dirty paws on me I'll beat your stupid brains out!"

He hauled up short, startled and surprised. Nancy backed along the wall, watching him, knowing that she had meant exactly what she'd said. She'd fight him as long as there was breath in her body, no matter what the consequences. They could kill her — they'd have to kill her — because she'd never willingly do anything they tried to make her do.

She reached the bed, and edged around it. If she could get her hands on that heavy, cast-iron chamber pot . . .

But she didn't make it. He rushed like a bull as she edged along before the bed.

He wanted to bowl her back upon it, she knew. He wanted to close with her.

She threw herself to the floor as he rushed, and one of his knees caught her, accidentally, on the side of the head.

Its force was terrific. She saw flashing, brassy lights before her eyes, and tasted brass in her mouth. The room reeled, and for a moment, her senses swam. But she never forgot her objective, and, flat on the floor, half unconscious, she reached under the bed and seized the handle of the thing.

Rolling back, she pulled it out. And now, when she needed them, her senses began to clear, and her fury burned with a bright, sharp flame.

She fought to her knees and up to her feet. Alf had sprawled clear across the bed, his head slamming into the adobe wall. He turned on his back and came up to a sitting position, and as he did, Nancy took the pot, with both her hands on the wire handle, and swung it with every bit of her strength.

The heavy cast-iron pot, which weighed nearly ten pounds, struck him squarely on the forehead and glanced off.

It was like striking a deep-set, ancient fence post, because Alf didn't even move. His shaggy head didn't snap back, and he didn't fall back against the wall.

For an instant she thought she had wasted all her effort and had lost, but then she saw his eyes begin to glaze.

She raised the pot and slammed him, hard, again. And this time he tipped sideways and fell sprawled across the bed.

Nancy dropped the pot with a clatter. Her whole body began to shake, beginning with her knees and ending with her shoulders and arms and hands. As though she had a chill, she staggered across to the door and flung it wide.

All four of the Maxfields were watching the door in breathless fascination. Nancy said, "Come get that pig off my bed. I want to go to sleep."

With silent awe, they got up as one man and filed across towards her. They went into the room. Miles and Will got Alf's head and feet and carried him out like a sack of grain. Vic stood inside the door, looking stupidly first at Nancy and then at Alf. Ezra, a grin touching the corners of his thin mouth, kicked the chamber pot back under the bed with a crash.

They went out, and Nancy closed the door. She went over, flung the top cover off the bed and threw herself across it.

And she heard their laughter begin. It roared through the house in gales, mounting to a crescendo, fading, then mounting again.

Alf would hate her now. And when he got that quirt in his hand . . . Nancy forced that thought from her mind. From now on, she'd take just one thing at a time.

CHAPTER FOURTEEN

Luke was a little startled as he rode away from the ambush, startled at its complete success. He had thought it would be more difficult, had even doubted if he could pull it off.

He grinned grimly as he heard the wild shooting behind him, as Gabe emptied his gun into the night. His grin widened as he heard Gabe screaming curses at the sky, and he chuckled as he envisaged Gabe's fury at having to walk all the way back to the Holcomb place.

He had three full days now, and three full nights, in which to put distance between himself and the Maxfield clan. He could travel at a fairly leisurely pace and still leave them far behind. They'd follow for a while, all right, but a trail that is three days old is well nigh impossible to follow, particularly if a storm should even partially wipe it out.

He had faced the reality of certain death,

and now he faced the opposite, the virtual certainty of continuing life. Turning north, he let his horse travel at a walk in the direction of the bluff where he had left both his rifle and canteen.

He reached the place and climbed to the shelf afoot, taking his time. He retrieved his rifle and canteen and went back down the slope. He mounted and continued north.

There was still pain in his wounds, and weakness in his body, but they were less than they had been, in spite of his violent exertions tonight. Perhaps, he thought, some of his improvement was due to his state of mind, to the return of hope to his thoughts. Now he was facing life again, instead of facing death.

The miles dropped away slowly behind him, each one adding to his feeling of security. The episode of the Maxfields was finished. Luke would probably never see them again.

He had accomplished what he set out to do — he had killed Spence and revenged the Ortiz family. And now he could put it from his mind.

Where he would go and what he would do he didn't know. More aimless drifting, he supposed. More loneliness, but then he was used to that.

What he couldn't understand was why he didn't feel better about getting away. He ought to be glad it was over and well behind him. He ought to be thankful it had turned out as well as it had.

Travelling by night, exercising reasonable care, it was probable that he'd get through the Indian country safely. So he had no worries, no problems at all.

His mind kept returning to the Holcomb place and each time it did, he resolutely put it on something else. He didn't want to think about that lonely ranch back there or about Nancy Holcomb, alone and at the mercy of the Maxfields. They wouldn't hurt her, he told himself firmly. Even out here, where a man made most of his own law, they wouldn't dare touch a girl like her.

But even as he thought that, he knew he was lying to himself.

Well, it wasn't Luke's business. She'd let him know that plainly enough. He'd tried to help her, tried to get her away. But she hadn't wanted it that way. She'd insisted on leaving him and going back, even though she'd known if the Maxfields didn't kill her the Comanches would.

So why should he worry himself about her? She wasn't his problem. He'd done all he could for her.

Besides, she'd abandoned him. She'd run off and left him, hurt and weak, to shift for himself. He didn't owe her a goddam thing.

He told himself all these things, but he wasn't convinced. And gradually, as he rode, he realized that there was nothing ahead of him. All that mattered was behind.

He kept remembering her as he had first seen her, barefooted, plain . . . He remembered her eyes, and the way he had felt when he'd caught her body in his arms.

He pulled his horse to a halt. He dismounted and paced nervously back and forth.

His wounds were on the mend and he was a fool if he turned and went back. It would be like stepping voluntarily upon a beehive. The chances that he'd survive, alive, were no better than . . .

Furious at himself, he knew then what he was going to do. He was going back.

He turned his horse around, cursing himself in an even, steady voice. He headed the animal south, and now a vague excitement touched his mind. He would see her again. He might die, but he'd see her again. And though he didn't realize it immediately, he had put his life into a single course for the first time. The wandering, lonely years were behind.

Almost as he turned, the grey of dawn laid a pale streak along the eastern horizon. He had scarcely gone a mile before the land was light, before a few high clouds in the east turned pale salmon pink.

Had he not turned back, he would now have found a place to hide and stopped, to wait out the daylight hours. But he didn't stop and he didn't hide, other than to keep his horse travelling in the low-lying ground. He'd have to take his chances on being spotted by Comanches, because he couldn't lie around waiting for dark. He had to get back to the Holcomb place before Gabe Maxfield did, a feat he had made nearly impossible by travelling north all night.

With a fresh horse it would have been easy. With a worn-out one it was not.

All morning he rode, and stopped at last near noon to rest his weary horse. The animal drank listlessly from an alkali stream, and disinterestedly cropped a few mouthfuls of grass. Luke gave him an hour, and then he mounted again.

The vague excitement kept growing in him. He caught himself praying soundlessly that he would be in time.

Gabe Maxfield was nearly dead as he staggered into the yard. He collapsed, unconscious, before he reached the house, and the other five came running out and carried him in and laid him carefully down on a bed. They returned, then, to get Les, who was also unconscious, and Mart, who was dead. Les they took inside, but Mart was left in the shade of the house and covered with a blanket.

Will mounted a horse and rode along their backtrail, scouting. Not once did it occur to him that Gabe and the others had not run into Comanches. There had been three of them. It would have taken at least a dozen braves to hurt them this bad.

He rode for several miles without finding evidence of pursuing Comanches. Then he turned and rode back towards the house. Gabe must have hurt the war party as badly as the war party had hurt him. Else they'd have been on his trail.

And Gabe. He came to slowly, slow to realize that he had reached his objective. He tried to get up, but hands pushed him back. He stared stupidly up at the ring of faces around him for a moment before he recognized them as his brothers and knew he had made it back.

And now, memory of all that had happened came flooding to his mind. With it came renewed anger, and his old, implacable thirst for revenge.

Miles was asking, "What happened, Gabe? Injuns?"

Gabe shook his head.

"Then what, for God's sake?"

Gabe's voice was cracked, but it was venomous. "That son-of-a-bitchin' Partin!"

"You mean he did all this to you? Killed Mart, shot Les, an' put you all afoot?"

Gabe didn't answer. He saw the expressions on their faces and sat up furiously. "Not a goddam one of you would of done any better! That bastard is sly as a wolf."

"How'd it happen?"

Gabe told them, his narrative liberally sprinkled with four-letter expletives describing Partin. He sat up as he talked and drank at frequent intervals from the brown bottle Miles had handed him, wiping his mouth each time with the hairy back of his hand.

He kept staring at Nancy, who was cooking at the stove. And there was hate in his eyes, as though he blamed her for Partin's existence.

He finished off the bottle and threw it savagely against the wall, where it shattered noisily. Nancy jumped, startled, and Gabe roared at her, "Don't just stand there! Bring me somethin' to eat."

Pale-faced, she began to fill a plate. She

162

brought it to him silently and returned for coffee.

She knew what a dangerous position she was in. Gabe's fury had gone beyond the bounds of control. And if someone told him now that she had tried to escape . . .

She tried to be as unobtrusive as possible, tried to keep her expression blank. But she couldn't help the elation, the triumph that flooded over her heart. Hurt, outnumbered, Luke Partin had still managed to soundly defeat Gabe and Mart and Les.

She brought Gabe coffee, her eyes sparkling in spite of her determination not to show her elation. And for the first time since the Maxfields had taken over here, she began to feel a touch of hope.

Abruptly it faded and all the sparkle left her eyes. Luke Partin owed her nothing. She had treated him shabbily all the way along the line. And she had abandoned him out there alone while he was still unable to travel. He must be thinking that she had pointed the Maxfields straight to him.

The hope that had been born in her heart was gone, and there was nothing left for her. She'd fight, and she wouldn't let them break her, but it was a hopeless fight that she knew she couldn't win. Sooner or later one of them would completely lose control of himself and kill her. Maybe that one would be Gabe, and maybe it was nearer than she thought.

With her back to them, she worked steadily at the stove, trying not to make any noise. She didn't want to draw their attention now.

But she listened. To Will's question, "What now, Gabe?"

And to Gabe's sudden, explosive answer. "Goddam it, what do you mean, 'What now?' We go after the bastard, that's what!"

Ezra said tentatively, "Maybe the Comanches will get him."

Gabe whirled on him. "You son-of-a-bitch, what kind of talk is that? *We'll* get him! He's ours. He killed Spence an' now he's killed Mart. We'll get him if we have to trail him clear to Canada."

Nobody spoke. Gabe got up and glared furiously at them, one after the other, forcing each to drop his glance.

Will said calmly, "What about her? What about this ranch?"

"Les can watch her. We won't be gone over a week."

"What if . . ."

Gabe's voice rose to a shouting roar. "What if? What if? You damn yellowbellies, what if Comanches *do* come? Ezra can fix

164

up a marriage certificate, even if the girl's dead. We still get the ranch. Now go out and start saddling up. And pack enough grub to last a week. We're goin' to be ridin' fast, an' there won't be time to hunt."

Nancy felt a sodden emptiness in the pit of her stomach. To be left alone with Les, whom she knew to be the most dangerously sadistic of the lot . . .

But even this might turn out well. Les was hurt. Right now he was lying over there on the couch, only half conscious. He'd have to sleep a lot, and while he was asleep . . .

The Maxfields scattered each to make preparations to leave. And Gabe sat there staring at her moodily, dangerously, until she felt as though she wanted to sink through the floor.

CHAPTER FIFTEEN

Preparations went on for half an hour, but at last the horses were saddled and waiting out before the door. Each had a roll of blankets and provisions tied behind the saddle. Each had a rifle in the saddle boot, and a canteen hung from the horn.

Outside Miles shouted, "All ready, Gabe!"

Gabe went to the door. "That grave dug?"

"Yeah. On that knoll behind the house. Alf an' Vic are just finishin' up."

Gabe swung around. "Come on, Les." He looked at Nancy. "You stay here."

If there was grief in him, Nancy couldn't see it. She said, "Do you want a Bible?"

He shook his head, and for the first time, Nancy saw confusion in him. She said, "Ezra can read."

"No! Come on, Les." He went out the door, and Les hobbled along behind. All of the brothers, and Miles, dropped whatever they were doing. Gabe went over and picked up Mart, for all his size, in his arms, blanket and all. He carried him at a swift, unfaltering walk up the slope behind the house.

When Nancy could no longer see, she went to one of the back windows. The house was partly sunk into the slope, but the window was at ground level and she could see the grave and the men grouped around it. They were a savage, wild-looking lot, dirty, some of them ragged, and all unshaven. Their hair, long and uncombed, looked strange bared to the sky. They held their hats awkwardly in their calloused, powerful hands, and looked at Gabe with subdued eyes.

Nancy opened the window. Mart's body, still blanket covered, lay at the side of the grave. The rocky earth that had been taken out of it was piled on the other side.

Gabe, hat in hand, said, "Mart here was likely the best of us all. He was a good hand with horses an' dogs, I can say that for him. He was a sight better'n Spence, that's certain, but he was killed by the same man. We're goin' after that man right now, an' we ain't goin' to stop until he's dead. Alf there, he wants the girl, an' some of us wants this ranch, an' I reckon Ezra would like to have that gold when we find it. But it's all got to wait."

He stooped and got hold of Mart's two hands. Nancy shuddered slightly. Rigor mortis had stiffened the body, and he couldn't raise them. So he took hold of the blanket, spread it out, then gently lifted Mart's body onto it. He said, "Get the corners an' we'll lower him in."

Three of the others, Vic and Alf and Will, each took a corner of the blanket. Then, awkwardly but gently, they lowered the body into the grave.

They stood up then and Gabe put on his hat. He nodded to Vic and Alf, who picked up their shovels and began to fill the grave.

All the Maxfields stood solemn and unmoving until the job was done. Then they tramped back towards the house.

Gabe came in first, closely followed by Les who immediately crossed the room and eased himself down on the couch.

Gabe's glance rested steadily on Nancy's face. "You take care of Les. Understand? If you don't . . ." He left the sentence dangling threateningly.

From the door, Will said, "What if she tries to get away again?"

Gabe's eyes flared. "What do you mean, again?"

"She tried it once while you were gone."

Gabe crossed the room to Nancy. His

hand swung suddenly, savagely, and struck the side of her face with an impact that nearly knocked her down.

Nancy's eyes flared. For the first time in her life she wanted to kill, and it showed plainly in her eyes. Gabe shouted, "You sure as hell need some breakin', you little bitch, and I'm just the one that can do the job. If I wasn't in a hurry, I'd give you that quirtin' I promised you right now."

Nancy didn't speak. She only hated him virulently with her eyes.

Alf, who had come in behind Will, said vengefully, "It wouldn't take long, Gabe. Let's do it now. Just gimme five minutes with a quirt in my hand an' by God she won't be so uppity next time."

Gabe swung his shaggy head. All the others had crowded in the door, their faces expectant. All of them except Alf were grinning. His eyes, small and piggish, were as hard as pieces of ice.

Will chuckled slyly. "She hit Alf with a chamber pot, Gabe. For practically nothin', too. All he wanted was to get in bed with her."

"I thought I told you . . ." Gabe stopped. He stood clenching his fists silently for a moment. "Hell, don't nobody listen to nothin'?" He spoke disgustedly towards the door. "Get mounted. I'll catch up."

He stared across the room at Les, doubt in his eyes, uncertainty in the way he stood.

Nancy could tell that he was weighing Les's disability against his nature and wondering if she would be safe with him. He plainly hated to leave anyone who was able to ride and fight behind to watch Les, but neither did he want Nancy hurt or killed.

The others had gone out, but Will still lounged in the door. His eyes were steady as he voiced Gabe's own doubts. "You better leave someone else or she won't be here when we get back. You know what Les is like. He'll have some story like he had with Rafael . . ."

"He'd better not. Go on, get started."

Will went out. Mumbling to himself, Gabe crossed the room to Les, who was watching him with pain-filled eyes and lying gingerly on his side.

Gabe said, "You let her alone or I'll kill you myself."

Les just stared at him. After a few moments Gabe shouted, "Damn you, I mean it. I'll kill you with my own two hands."

He turned away, something like disgust in his eyes as he remembered all the animals Les had crippled and killed. He stared at

Nancy as he went towards the door. "You'd better *both* be here. Understand?"

She nodded. She didn't intend to be, but neither did she intend to antagonize him further.

She heard them as they mounted and pounded out of the yard. She headed for the door to watch them leave. Les's voice, soft and deadly, stopped her. "Don't go near that door."

She turned her head. He had a revolver in his hand and the hammer was cocked.

She backed away from the door. She hadn't missed the direction the gun was pointed. Not at her body, but at her legs below the knees. She shuddered visibly.

He eased carefully off the bed on to his hands and knees. Then he got up.

He walked towards her painfully, limping. There was a five- or six-day growth of whiskers on his face, which was also covered with a thick layer of dust and sweat. She noticed that his eyes were almost the colour of a baby's eyes, greyish blue, an odd shade, and possessed a strange brightness. He said, "Gabe told me not to hurt you but Gabe's gone. So stay in the house. Maybe I can't run very fast, but I'm one hell of a good shot."

Nancy backed as far as she could until

her back was against the stove. Les followed her, that peculiar light growing in his eyes.

Then, as abruptly as it had grown, it faded and disappeared. His thoughts had gone elsewhere. He limped to the door and stood leaning against the jamb, staring north in the direction his father and brothers had gone.

He glanced at her over his shoulder, grinning at the whiteness of her face, at the way the pulses jumped in her throat. "They'll kill Partin slow," he said, "like Injuns do. Nobody does us like he's done. Nobody!"

Nancy said, "Maybe he'll do your father and five brothers like he did you three. He's . . ."

"Shut up! Shut your goddam mouth and keep it shut."

Nancy did. She couldn't afford to stir him up. She realized how unstable he was, how unpredictably dangerous. She would have to treat him with extreme care if she were going to get that chance she wanted to escape. Sooner or later he'd tire, and when he did . . .

She said, "Do you want something to eat?"

He nodded, still staring out at the empty plain. Nancy fixed a plate and took it to him. And again, as he took it from her, that odd light returned to his eyes.

It always made her shudder, for she sensed what put it there. He was thinking of all the things he would like to do to her. She backed away. Les took the plate to the table, put it down, and began to eat standing up.

A feeling of helpless discouragement came over Nancy. She almost wished they had done whatever they intended doing to her. She couldn't stand much more of this waiting, this awful terror. She didn't know how long she could fence with Les, a crazed killer if ever there was one. She dreaded the coming of night.

So Luke was gone, and she had to accept that fact. There was no help coming for her. She was on her own.

Les would tie her up at night. It was the only way he could sleep and be sure she wouldn't get away. And while she was helplessly tied . . .

Her chest felt as though it were full of ice.

Les finished eating. He picked up a brown bottle half full of whisky from the table and took a drink.

All the time, his eyes had been on her, clinging as tenaciously, as terrifyingly as a pair of leeches. He wiped his mouth with the back of his hand and proffered the bottle. "Drink, girlie?"

Nancy shook her head. She'd run before

173

she'd let him touch her, and no ruse like offering her a drink would get her close to him. She'd risk his expert marksmanship. Better to be shot than to let him . . .

His eyes began to burn, but there was still a certain caution in them. She could tell he was thinking of Gabe and of Gabe's threat.

But how long would Gabe's threat deter him? Its potency would fade with time. Les would tell himself that he wasn't even sure Gabe was coming back. He would tell himself that Gabe, faced with something already done and beyond recall, might forget his threat. He would work himself up to a pitch where there was no self-control. Will had mentioned Rafael. She didn't know who Rafael was, but apparently from the way Will had spoken, it was someone they suspected Les had killed.

Les hobbled towards her, and she backed away. He stopped and took another drink from the bottle — a long one.

Nancy didn't know whether his drinking would save her or doom her. If he drank too much he might pass out, giving her the chance she needed. On the other hand, a little whisky might only make him more dangerous.

Suddenly she bolted for her bedroom, slammed and bolted the door. She heard his footsteps approaching it, heard him rattle the knob and try breaking it open with his shoulder.

Then he began to laugh. "I'll get in when I'm ready, girlie. All I got to do is shoot off the bolt. But right now I'm goin' to finish this bottle and take me a little nap."

Nancy sat down weakly on the edge of the bed. He was playing a cruel game with her now. He'd go on making noises out there for a while, and then all would be utterly and completely still. He'd want her to think he was sleeping, but when she opened the door and came out . . .

There was only one chance for her. She'd find some kind of weapon, if only a chair, and she'd fight as hard as she could. She'd either make him kill her quickly, or she'd get away.

CHAPTER SIXTEEN

It had been about nine when the Maxfields left. It was now about nine-thirty. Nancy sat on the edge of the bed, staring emptily at the door.

The end was near. She'd play Les Maxfield's little game. Only when she came out through that door, it wouldn't be quietly, stealthily, in the belief he was asleep. She'd come through running, with some kind of weapon in her hand.

With luck she could make it through the outside door before he recovered from his surprise. Then she'd find out how good a shot he was. Because he'd have to shoot her. Nothing else would make her stop.

Thinking of what she was going to do made her heart beat fast, made her hands and her knees tremble violently. Damn them! Damn them for what they'd done to her! If she could get to a town — somewhere there must be people who would take a stand, no matter how many Maxfields there were. Someplace she'd find decent people, and law, and then they would pay and she'd have her ranch again, and this home, though she doubted if she'd want to live in it again, so strong would be the memory of all that had happened here.

Deliberately she turned her thoughts from herself and what she must do in the next few minutes and thought of Luke Partin, trying to steady herself. She should have stayed with him, and now she wished she had. She found herself remembering his face, so competent and sure, and yet with a brooding loneliness about it she'd never quite understood.

A man who did the things that had to be done, whatever they happened to be. A man much like her father had been, like Ben would have been if he'd lived. A man strong enough to run this ranch, and make it pay. A man who would have strong sons . . .

She flushed at the intimate way her thoughts had turned. She was a fool. Luke Partin was gone and would never return. She'd had her chance and had turned it down because she wouldn't listen to him or even trust him. But if she had trusted, and if she had listened — why even now they'd be travelling across the northern plain. With days, maybe weeks, alone with him she'd have made him want her, no matter what she had to do. You didn't get a man by fighting him, and deserting him when he needed you.

But it was too late now. Too late for anything except, maybe, saving her life.

Out in the other room all was quiet, just as she had known it would be. She could almost see Les waiting there beside the door, breathing softly, as patient as a cat waiting beside a mouse's hole. She must give him time to get tired of waiting, so that he'd be off guard. But not too much time or he'd lose his patience and begin to shoot at the bolt.

She began to count slowly. Sixty to a minute. Five minutes, ten.

Silently now she got up. The cast-iron chamber pot was gone, the one she had knocked Alf out with. But there was a china water pitcher half filled with water to give it weight. If she hit him squarely in the face with that. . . .

She picked it up silently and crossed to the door. She knew the sound the bolt made when it was drawn back, but she also knew that by pushing against the door as she drew it, she could avoid any sound at all.

Doing so, she cautiously pulled it back.

The door was unlocked now. All she must do was fling it open and dart on through.

For a moment, she thought she couldn't do it. She couldn't fight a man like Les and win. She was only a woman.

Then she thought of the things Les had in mind for her. She couldn't know exactly what they were, but she did know they were ugly and horrible and would probably end in death. She thought of Luke Partin, and of the way he had sent the three Maxfields back, one dead, one hurt, the other walking and leading a wounded horse. If he could do that, she could certainly do this. She flung open the door and darted through.

As she had expected, Les was waiting beside the door. But he wasn't expecting her and was lounging against the wall, relaxed, grinning expectantly.

She caught him completely by surprise. He started violently, then shoved himself away from the wall and lunged for her.

She whirled to face him, realizing how close he was, startled at how quickly he recovered from his surprise. He'd bring her down if he flung himself straight out in a dive and clutched at her lower legs.

He dived for her and she brought the pitcher down, holding it in both hands, nearly paralysed with fear but desperately hoping it would strike his head.

It did, and smashed into small pieces. Water cascaded over Les, splashing on Nancy herself.

She didn't wait to see what effect her blow had. She turned and fled towards the door.

Out into the brilliant sunshine and across the dusty yard towards the corral. Breathlessly she hoped no Comanches were in the area, that they were not watching the house. Because Comanches or no, she couldn't stay.

She made it to the corral before she dared to look behind. Each foot of the way across the yard, she had expected shots from the house, had expected bullets to tear into her legs. Now she looked around and saw that the door was still empty, still gaping open.

With trembling hands, she found a rope and caught herself a horse. Then, fashioning a hackamore with the rope, she led the horse out and flung herself to his back. Lying low across his withers, she thundered away, drumming against his sides with her heels.

She looked behind again from three hundred yards, just as she pounded over a rise. The door was still empty.

She heaved a shaky sigh of relief. She had hit him harder than she'd expected to, or he would have recovered by now. He'd come to all right and would take her trail at once. But wounded as he was, he'd have a hard time keeping up. With luck, she ought to get away.

But there was one thing Nancy didn't see. Half a mile from the house an Indian moved, easing silently back from his vantage point on moccasined feet. He got his horse, mounted, and took Nancy's trail.

An hour before sundown, Luke Partin caught sight of the house. He dismounted not far from where the Indian had been and eased forward afoot. From here he watched the house steadily, unmovingly, for almost half an hour. The door hung open, swinging slightly in the breeze. Half a dozen horses drowsed in the corral, through a corner of which a small stream of water flowed. One of them listlessly nuzzled a pile of wild hay that had been almost trampled into the ground.

Otherwise, nothing moved. No wisp of smoke drifted from the chimney.

Luke went back and got his horse, uneasiness stirring him. Either the place was deserted or the Maxfields, in some way knowing of his approach, had set a nasty trap.

He doubted the latter possibility. He doubted if anyone could possibly know he was headed here. Nor did he think the place had been attacked by Indians, for they would have burned it to the ground.

He circled cautiously, while the sun sank lower and lower in the west. And at last he rode out on the knoll behind the house.

Again he stopped, but this time he did not dismount. Nothing had changed about the scene below, and still nothing stirred. Luke rode down the knoll.

Nervously he watched those high, narrow windows in the rear of the house. And fifty yards away from the house, he found Mart's grave. His horse sidestepped it.

He dismounted immediately behind the house and dropped his reins. Then, gun in hand, crouching a little, he ran around the house.

From the corner, he watched the front door for a moment. Uneasiness was in him, and a cold, crawling feeling was in his spine. This was eerie. The Maxfields would not have taken Nancy with them when they rode north after him. And besides, one of them had been hurt in a spot that would make it impossible for him to ride very far, if at all.

He heard no sound and saw no movement, and so, after a few moments, he charged in through the door.

Halfway across the room he skidded to a halt. All was silent and nothing moved. He went through the house swiftly, conscious of the fading light outside. He found the fragments of the shattered pitcher, and a few drops of blood, and that was all.

Quickly he went outside. He took time to scan the four horizons minutely before he began to quarter across the yard, searching the ground carefully.

He found her tracks almost at once and knew she had been running hard. Following them, he found that they led directly to the corral. Here, he picked up the tracks of two horses, also running hard and heading out towards the southeast. The tracks of one of the horses occasionally overlaid those of the other, making it obvious that she had been pursued.

By the wounded Les, he supposed. All the others had apparently ridden north in search of Luke himself.

He went back to the house and got his horse. Pushing hard and increasingly conscious of the fading light, he rode along the trail she had left.

He travelled almost two miles before the tracks of a third horse fell into the trail of the other two. He didn't even need to dismount to know who this third horseman had been. An Indian, riding an unshod, untrimmed horse.

He went on, necessarily slowed now because the sky was growing dark. And at last, five miles from the house, he was forced to stop.

He sat there gloomily for a long moment. Probably Nancy Holcomb was no longer alive. He forced himself to accept the probability, a little surprised at the sense of loss he felt, a little surprised at the anger that rose so unexpectedly in his heart.

Hounded like an animal, hunted, she had shown a courage he had somehow felt she would possess. She had obviously knocked Les out with that pitcher. And then she'd fled.

Regretfully, Luke turned and rode back towards the house, arriving as first full dark came across the land.

Again he approached cautiously, for he knew if there had been one Indian in the vicinity, there could have been others. But the house was still deserted.

First, he lighted a lamp and found food for himself, which he wolfed down hungrily. By the time he had finished, the fire he had built in the stove had boiled the cold coffee left in the pot. He drank three cups before his hunger for the stuff was sated.

Then he went outside to the corral. He took considerable time here, selecting the best horse. When he was satisfied that he had done so, he saddled the animal and led him towards the house.

He thought grimly that the Maxfields would love this when they returned, having the man they sought come here in their absence and eat and drink and take a fresh horse, the best of the lot.

Inside, Luke got a couple of extra blankets and rolled up inside them provisions enough to last him more than a week. He also found powder and lead and percussion caps to replenish his dwindling supply.

Before he blew out the lamp, he stopped and stared around at the interior of the place. It was untidy now, but then any place the Maxfields stayed would be that. But it was snug and tight and safe. A man and woman could defend it against almost anything the Indians could throw against it.

Its walls were more than two feet thick, of solid adobe. Its ceiling was made of log beams, and he knew that on top of them was a couple of feet of sod. Windows were high enough to admit light, yet narrow enough to prevent the entrance of a man.

And the door. The door was of solid oak planks two inches thick and strapped with wrought iron.

As nearly impregnable as Holcomb could make it, it had a cellar beneath it that stored enough supplies to keep a family for more than a month. And now he must leave it open, unguarded, an invitation to the Comanches to destroy it.

He blew out the lamp and closed the door behind him, dropping the bar into place by means of the rawhide latchstring. He mounted the horse he had saddled and rode away into the night.

He headed directly for the place where darkness had made him lose the trail, reaching it about a half hour later. Here, he dismounted and picketed his horse. Then he wrapped himself in his blankets and lay down on the ground.

As tired as he was, as close to exhaustion, he still did not sleep immediately but instead stared moodily up at the stars. He supposed he had been a fool to come back, for his return had accomplished nothing. Tomorrow he would find the place where Nancy Holcomb had been captured by Comanches. Probably he would find her body there.

It hurt to think of that. It hurt to think of

her dying, in pain and terror. It hurt to think of her dead.

But he swore one thing. If Nancy Holcomb was dead, he would make the Maxfields pay for the crime. He would do that if nothing else.

CHAPTER SEVENTEEN

He awoke half an hour before dawn and rose immediately. He saddled and packed his horse, except for the lead he had taken from the Holcomb place, and his bullet mould.

As soon as it was beginning to get light, he built a small fire and put the lead on the fire in a pan. Then he squatted beside the fire, waiting for it to melt.

He was not thinking of the Maxfields now. He was thinking of Nancy Holcomb, and trying to recall each expression she had worn, each thing she had said.

Her voice had been pleasant, soft and low and warm. Her eyes, which had made him realize that she was truly beautiful in spite of his first impression of plainness, had been wide-spaced, calm — but they had possessed a way of sparkling with sudden anger.

And he knew she might still be alive — captive of Comanches perhaps, but then women had been recaptured from them before. Some of them, though cruelly treated, had recovered from their experiences and lived long and happy lives.

Nancy would be like these, he knew. There was iron in her, strength that would prevent them from breaking her.

The melting of the lead was maddeningly slow, but he waited with seemingly stolid patience. In the hours ahead he would need bullets, perhaps a lot of them. And a few minutes spent equipping himself now were well spent.

It melted at last, and he poured his bullets carefully, dumping the cool ones out on the ground, pouring more, until at last the lead was gone.

He gathered up the bullets and put them in his pouch. He stowed the pan behind his saddle. He returned the bullet mould to his saddlebags.

Then he mounted and rode away upon the trail he had been forced to abandon last night.

He did not regret having returned. He realized it was the only thing he could have done — and lived with himself afterwards. Nancy Holcomb dominated his thoughts, and he knew she would always remain there.

Never before had a woman so deeply

impressed him, never before had he wanted one as he wanted Nancy. He admitted to himself a trifle ruefully that he might well be deluding himself. He had reached an age when the urge to make a home became strongest in a man.

But there was more to it than that, an instinctive feeling, perhaps, that told him Nancy Holcomb was the one he had to have.

Watchful, quiet-faced, he rode the trail, dividing his attention between it and the surrounding terrain. The high clouds turned pink and a glow grew stronger immediately above the eastern rim of the plain.

Suddenly, he saw ahead the specks of buzzards circling, diving in to land. Something was dead, and for a moment Luke halted, his fists clenched tight against the pommel of the saddle between his knees.

Nancy Holcomb — or Les Maxfield? Or an Indian? He spurred on, lifting the horse to a hard, fast run.

No need for stealth. Buzzards would not have settled had there been anything living nearby.

The miles ran swiftly beneath the pounding hoofs of his horse. A dust cloud raised, following him on the slight breeze from the south.

The sun came up, immediately hot as it laid its rays against his side. He tilted his hat against it and squinted, straining his eyes ahead.

And then, at last, the scene he had been waiting for — brown, ugly birds with red necks and heads like turkeys, with ugly wattles hanging down, walking around awkwardly, rending, tearing, quarrelling.

They rose with a thunderous flapping as Luke pounded up, and as they cleared the ground the horror of suspense died and he knew who it was that lay there nearly torn apart. It was Les Maxfield.

Luke's horse shied violently as the smell of death drifted to him on an eddy of the wind. Luke swung down, stooping to tie the horse to a deep-rooted clump of brush.

He walked slowly towards the body on the ground, distaste in his face, a quiet horror in his eyes.

Les Maxfield had been stripped of his clothes. He had been staked out flat, belly up. His tongue was gone, as were his genitals, and a fire had been built on his stomach.

Luke knew it had taken Les Maxfield a long, long time to die. Perhaps most of the night his screams had ripped through the still, dark air, at least until they tired of his screams and cut his tongue out.

He turned away from the body, repressing a shudder of disgust. He began to circle, his lips moving soundlessly. If Nancy was dead, she would be close by.

He circled in ever-widening circles until he was two hundred yards from the body on the ground. He searched in each small draw, behind each clump of brush. He beat through a mesquite thicket, searching it thoroughly. But he found nothing.

He returned to the place he had left his horse. He mounted and this time made a wider circle, watching the ground for tracks. He had nearly completed the circle before he found them.

He dismounted and squatted, studying the ground. He counted six unshod Indian horses. He saw the prints of Nancy's horse, and these he studied long and hard. Were the prints less deep than they would be if the horse was carrying Nancy's weight? He couldn't say definitely, for the ground was hard. He saw the prints of Les's horse overlying the others, indicating the horse had been trailed behind.

The tracks led north and slightly west. Luke mounted and followed, his eyes studying but one of the sets of tracks, those of Nancy's horse.

He rode for several miles, ascertaining definitely the direction the Indians were taking, satisfying himself that it was the true direction they intended to go and not a false trail from which they would deviate farther on. Then he stopped and dismounted and hunkered down on the ground, scowling.

He must reach a decision now. He must make a choice. He knew there was little chance of his being able to rescue Nancy. She was captive of at least six Comanches, who seemed to be heading towards their camp. How large that camp would be, Luke couldn't tell, but it probably contained several hundred people. In all probability, the six braves who had captured Nancy would reach it before Luke caught up with them.

Several choices were open to him. He could return to Comanche Wells, the nearest town, and try to enlist help, though his chance of doing so was slim. The town feared the Maxfields and knew they were after Luke. Few of the men would be interested in taking on the Maxfields and the Comanches both for a girl they didn't even know.

There was another choice — the ranger barracks two hundred miles away. An even poorer choice, for it would be several days before he could reach the place and return with help.

Discarding both these choices left him with an even less hopeful third alternative. The Maxfields themselves. They wouldn't help voluntarily but . . . A desperate gamble, the only answer he could think of for the desperate situation facing him.

For a long, long time he squatted there, staring out across the baking land with narrowed eyes. His mind was considering all the angles involved in the plan he had in mind.

The chances of its success were poor. Everything must work out exactly or nothing would come out right in the end. And Luke had lived long enough to know that few things work out exactly as they are planned.

Yet he had no better plan. So he got up, mounted, and again set out on the Indians' trail.

It continued in a straight northwesterly direction. He rode for the better part of the morning, pushing his horse to the limit of his endurance. Occasionally he checked the trail he followed, but mostly his eyes were upon the horizon, watching for tell-tale clouds of lifting dust, or movement, or colour not natural to the landscape.

On into the afternoon without stopping. Now the body of Les Maxfield lay twenty miles behind, and off to his right somewhere, trailing, the six remaining Maxfields rode.

But the Indian camp was first. He had to know exactly where it was, and guessing wouldn't do.

He rode more cautiously as the hours passed, and more slowly too. Whenever possible, he abandoned the trail altogether and rode for several miles in a draw or sink, hidden from the stretch of open land.

At last, in late afternoon, he spotted it, by a haze of smoke and dust rising faintly into the clear blue air ahead of him. And now he turned at right angles and rode along the south side of a bluff and up on top of it. He tied his horse in a clump of mesquite and carefully crawled to the rim of the bluff, from which point he could look down on the Comanche village.

He counted the tepees of bleached buffalo hide — nearly a hundred in all. Five people to a tepee was a good average. Five hundred people, of which perhaps a hundred would be fighting men.

He crawled back carefully so that his movement would not be visible to a chance watcher below. Once out of sight, he ran to his horse, mounted and picked his way down off the bluff.

And now he rode due east as hard as his horse could go. He had to find the Maxfields' trail before nightfall.

His horse, in spite of the hard ride today, was still fairly fresh — fresher by far than Luke's own horse had been since leaving the Ortiz house pursuing Spence. He was tired, but his wounds were far less painful than they had been before.

Risking discovery, he rode without attempt at concealing himself. For he knew that unless he found the Maxfields tonight, his plan would have practically no chance of even partial success.

The hours passed and the miles fell regularly behind. The sun sank lower and lower in the west. Luke began to think he had miscalculated distance or direction, when all at once he came over a long ridge and saw, ahead of him, the cave where he had made camp.

Here he'd find the beginning of the Maxfields' trail. Here he would know if he had a chance of catching them.

He grinned wryly at the irony of the situation. The Maxfields were pursuing him, but he was also pursuing them.

He headed straight towards the foot of the

slope above which was the overhang that had sheltered him. He watched the ground intently. He crossed trails, those of Gabe and Mart and Les, his own, but he did not find that of the six remaining members of the clan.

Caution touched him immediately and he stopped, taking time to scan the horizons in all directions. He saw nothing, and so began a large circle north of the overhang in the hopes of picking up their tracks there.

The sun hung low in the western sky. He estimated that less than three hours of daylight remained. How hard had they ridden, and how fast? How far north of here were they? They had been on the trail almost twenty-four hours longer than he had. But had there been time for them to follow north to the place he had turned back, and return this far?

His best bet, he guessed, was to find his own trail, the one he had made returning towards the Holcomb place. And backtrack that.

Accordingly he abandoned his search for the Maxfields' trail and headed out across the plain at a fast gallop. And now he did not have to watch the ground, for he knew he would recognize landmarks when he reached the place he had passed.

The sun sank lower and lower in the sky. The remaining hours of daylight dwindled fast.

But at last he came to a wide, dry stream bed, running along the foot of a rocky escarpment, and here he found his tracks, deeply indented in the hard, dry sand.

Tracks of a solitary horseman, himself, with no pursuers' tracks obliterating them. He turned north with faint hope touching his heart, with doubtful eyes on the setting sun. Time was running out. But he had reached this point before the Maxfields did, and they could not now be far away.

Good sense and caution would dictate now that he stop and conceal himself and watch. But there wasn't time. An hour, perhaps a little more, was all that was left of the light.

So he rode north, backtracking his own plain trail and pushing his tiring horse to the limit of its speed.

How far he went he didn't know. But at last, as the sky grew deep slate grey and objects less than half a mile away began to fade, he saw them come pounding over the top of a ridge not more than a mile away, silhouetted against the greying sky.

He didn't stop. They had not seen him. And until they did . . .

His horse thundered on. And the gap separating him from the Maxfields narrowed swiftly.

Half a mile, a quarter mile. And suddenly as he climbed out of an arroyo, he heard a shout dimmed by distance, "Gabe! Look there!"

He whirled his horse, rearing. Would they recognize him and pursue? If they didn't . . .

But if he flung a shot at them — that would leave no doubt in their minds. He snatched his rifle from the boot. He eased back the hammer and let it fall, sighting carefully above their heads at the greying sky.

The sound of the shot echoed back from a high rock face a quarter mile away. And Luke turned. Leaving this trail, he thundered away to the west with the six Maxfields in shouting, eager pursuit.

CHAPTER EIGHTEEN

Rapidly now, all remaining light faded from the sky. Luke rode low against his horse's withers, glancing often behind, straining his ears for sounds of pursuit.

He wondered what they would think about the happenstance of coming on him returning over the same route he had travelled several days before. He wondered if their suspicions would be aroused or if, jubilant over discovering him, they wouldn't give it any particular thought.

Suspicious they might be, but he doubted if they would grasp his plans for them, would suspect that he had deliberately showed himself to them so that they would chase him exactly where he wanted them to.

He lost the sound of pursuit momentarily and pulled his horse to a halt. Then he picked it up again and went on, making plenty of noise crashing through brush pockets and mesquite thickets, or thundering over rocky ground.

It would be a touchy thing, leading them all night long, staying exactly far enough ahead so that they wouldn't lose him and yet avoiding capture. It would be difficult to arrive at a given spot at a given hour in the morning.

But he didn't dare arrive at the Indian village before daylight tomorrow. There had to be light when he arrived.

Nor could the horses long sustain the pace at which they were now travelling. Sooner or later both he and the Maxfields would have to slow down or their horses would collapse beneath them. Yet Luke knew that as long as they could hear him, as long as they could follow they would do so, even if they killed their horses doing it.

So he deliberately drew ahead of them after a couple of hours of hard riding. The sounds of pursuit faded and died behind.

Luke rode on for another quarter mile and then stopped to rest his horse. He didn't dare unsaddle, but he did dismount and loosen up the cinch. He listened intently, trying to guess what they would do.

They were not fools. He guessed that as soon as they were sure they had lost him, they'd do exactly what he had done. They'd stop, and rest their mounts, and then come on, only not in a group this time. They'd separate, fan out, in spite of the obvious danger that he'd ambush them one by one. Luke guessed that Gabe Maxfield was willing to risk the lives of either his brothers or himself at this point in the case if only he could catch and kill the man who had already killed two of his brothers, who had made fools out of the rest at every turn.

So Luke waited, silent, listening, his hand on his horse's cinch. He wanted the horse to rest as long as he possibly could. But he didn't want to be caught unawares.

Minutes passed, dragging. Uneasiness touched Luke's mind, but he forced himself to wait and instead of relying only on his ears, watched those of his horse. The horse would detect the Maxfields' approach long before Luke did. And he'd show it by turning his head towards the approaching sound, by pricking his ears forward.

A light haze lay over the stars, diffusing their light rather than obliterating it. From a far-away hill a pack of coyotes yipped and quarrelled, to be answered by another, nearer in. A hunting hawk swooped low.

Luke's horse stiffened and turned his head. His ears pricked forward nervously. Luke immediately tightened up the cinch and swung astride.

A shape loomed against the sky on his right, another on his left. Damning the horse for waiting too long to turn his head and prick his ears — the animal *must* have heard them before he showed that he did — Luke gouged the animal's sides angrily with his spurs.

The horse lunged across a draw and up the slope on the far side. And a shot blazed out behind.

One of the Maxfields yelled triumphantly. "Here he is, Gabe!" and behind Luke the hoofs of two separate horses beat rapidly against the ground.

Luke reined over recklessly to the right, executing a wide, complete circle before he straightened out. For a few moments he was hidden by the draw, and then he was right in the midst of them and could hear them coming fast from both sides.

Gabe yelled, "Which way did he go?" And another answered from up ahead, "Back — we lost him — but he's here someplace. Shut up, everybody. Shut up and listen for him!"

Luke hauled his horse to an immediate halt. He could hear the hard, fast breathing of one of the Maxfields' mounts less than a dozen yards to his left.

His hands were shaking and his knees trembled slightly. How the hell was he going to get out of this? How the hell, without getting his brains blown out?

That one on his left yelled, "Sing out, each one of you! There's someone up ahead of me."

Gabe bawled from somewhere in the night, "I'm here, an' Pa's with me!"

From behind Luke Ezra yelled, "I'm here!"

Luke whirled his horse and pounded directly towards the one on his left.

A revolver flashed in the man's hand. And then Luke was past him and other guns were flaring in the night.

The same voice yelled furiously, "Goddam it, quit shootin'! You're shootin' straight at me!"

"Which way did he go?"

"This way. Of all the supid!"

But Luke was gone, not up the slope this time to be skylined at its top, but up the draw, hidden by thickets of mesquite and by the banks themselves. He didn't ride out until he reached a place where a low saddle led over the ridge.

They came on behind, their horses grouped again, talking and cursing savagely back and forth as they rode until Gabe roared authoritatively, "Shut up, the whole damn bunch of you! How the hell do you expect to follow him if you're yappin' like a pack of coyotes?"

Silence after that, and only the steady beat of hoofs. Luke's horse ran steadily, his breathing regular. Never again would he trust *this* horse, thought Luke. He'd rely on his own eyes and ears instead.

At midnight, he passed the place where he'd hidden out with Nancy Holcomb several days before. He detoured it and rode on, continuing his erratic, zigzagging course and trying to measure the miles in his mind against the hours of darkness remaining.

Arrive on a worn-out horse, trailing the Maxfields on horses in the same condition . . . There would be no escape from the trap Luke was going to spring. They would die at the hands of the Comanches, just as he would himself unless he had a more than generous supply of luck.

The minutes dragged, and the hours seemed like years. Luke tried desperately to pierce the darkness ahead, tried to see landmarks he had seen before. He tried to estimate what time it was and how soon it would be getting light.

There were moments when fear touched him — fear that he would miscalculate, that dawn would find him still far from the Indian village, or past it, virtually at the mercy of the Maxfields. He strained his eyes into the darkness, searching for landmarks he had seen only by daylight and so found it difficult to recognize at night.

At times the Maxfields drew dangerously close, and at times he had to slow and wait. But always he had to make it appear to them at least that he was doing his best to get away and not simply leading them in a given direction across the land, a thing that would have been impossible had not Luke's horse been far fresher and stronger than theirs.

At last he saw what he had been waiting for, a thin line of grey in the eastern sky, outlining the irregular horizon. And in its growing light, he recognized a bluff by which he had marked the Comanche camp ahead but far to his right.

Now began the touchiest part of the whole business. He must ride now in the low places, turning and dodging often to avoid being skylined at the top of some ridge. He must ride in places from which the Indian village would not be visible, and he could only hope that the Maxfields weren't closely watching the ground for tracks, plentiful this close to the Indians' camp.

He drew ahead slowly and did not hold back, for he knew they'd be able to see him in daylight at a much greater distance than they could hear him at night.

Only this lead permitted him the turns, the zigzagging, twisting course he took.

They did not always follow his turns. Sometimes they cut across instead of going the way that he had gone. He worried about the danger of that, but was doing the best he could. Besides, even if they saw the village, they would probably come on. Excitement had them all, and they were close enough to be certain of a kill. They knew it was only a matter of time before they'd run him down or wing him with a lucky shot.

Closer and closer he came to the Indian camp. And as he did, his nerves drew ever tighter. When he was less than a quarter mile away, just over a long low rise from the draw that held the village, he hauled his horse to a plunging halt, turned and emptied his revolver at the Maxfield clan.

They pulled up in complete surprise, from which they rapidly recovered. And they did what he had hoped they would. They began to fire at him recklessly.

The sound was like that of a small war, and Luke grinned tightly to himself. He whirled his horse, set his spurs, and pounded off up a small draw towards the north.

Nancy had ridden recklessly for several miles before she dared let her horse relax his running gait. When she did, at last, she swung her head and looked behind in time to sight the Indian who was following her coming over a ridge. He was more than a mile behind.

This was exactly what she had feared, but she didn't regret what she had done. To have remained at the house would have meant certain death, either at the hands of Les, or at the hands of Indians brought back by this one lone scout as soon as he was sure the ranch was guarded only by a girl and a wounded man. This way she was, at least, fighting back.

He seemed in no hurry and made no attempt to avoid being seen. He just maintained the distance between them, letting it grow neither wider nor narrower. By this she guessed that she was going in the direction he wanted her to, and that his companions were somewhere up ahead.

She changed her direction immediately, beginning a wide circle to the south. And the Indian followed suit, cutting across to head her off.

Seeing the distance between them steadily narrowing, she swung back to the north with a fatalistic shrug.

Now, far along her back trail, she glimpsed still another horseman, and guessed that this was Les. The Indian apparently saw Les at the same time she did, for he rode down into an arroyo and disappeared.

For a couple of hours, then, Nancy rode unmolested. And then, suddenly from a draw ahead, three Indians appeared riding at a gallop.

She whirled her horse and drummed on his sides, but it was no use. Before she had gone a mile she was overtaken and her horse caught and pulled to a halt.

She did not try to dismount and run, knowing how useless it would be. Instead she tried to retain her dignity and looked them in the faces as steadily as she could.

They rode away unhurriedly, the one who had caught her horse leading him, a specific destination apparently in their minds.

Glancing behind, Nancy failed to see Les and supposed the others of the party had captured him. They must have taken him completely by surprise, for she had heard no shots.

The Indians continued in a northerly direction for several hours, until the sun was halfway down the western sky, at which time they rode down on to a little flat where three others waited. Les Maxfield was staked out on the ground. He was naked, but he wasn't dead. He wouldn't look at her.

The Indian who had captured her dragged her off her horse with brutal savagery. Nancy didn't fight, even when he threw her to the ground. She knew if she angered him, he would probably go ahead and kill her outright.

He tied her feet with strips of rawhide and left her lying in the sun. Then he and his comrades grouped around Les's body on the ground, their black eyes gleaming, their swarthy faces glistening with sweat.

Nancy rolled, so that her back was to the scene. She couldn't see what they did to Les, but she could hear his tortured screams.

Her stomach churned. There were times when she thought she was going to faint. The sun sank lower and lower in the west, but still Les Maxfield didn't die.

Occasionally, the smoke from the fire they had built drifted towards her. Occasionally she smelled the sickening odour of scorching flesh.

She fainted at last, from the sun, from terror, from the sounds that she heard and the smells she smelled. She didn't know it when they tied her on a horse a few minutes after Les had died. She didn't feel the ride to the Indian camp. She did not regain consciousness until morning when one of the braves dumped her on the ground in front of his lodge and threw a skin of water into her face.

She was dragged into a tepee and dumped, still tied, at the rear of it. A squaw, perhaps ten years older than she, tied her hands angrily with strips of rawhide, so tight that her hands began to hurt almost immediately. Leaving, the squaw reviled her in the Comanche tongue, and spat on her.

From this, Nancy understood why she had not been killed when they caught her. One of the braves wanted her as his squaw. And this one, his present squaw, hated her because he did.

Why she had not been mistreated prior to their arrival in the village was also plain to her. At first they had been busy with Les. By the time Les had died, she had been unconscious.

So she faced, instead of a lifetime married to Alf Maxfield, a lifetime married to a Comanche brave. Her children would be half Indian. She might, in time, become almost Indian herself.

She would be treated cruelly for a while — beaten regularly by the displaced squaw. She would be forced to do all the hardest, most distasteful work there was. She would be given too little to eat and nothing but rags to wear.

But she would not be killed. And she would not be tortured. If she could endure the rest, a time of rescue might eventually come. Other women had been saved from captivity by the Indians. And maybe she might be too.

They did not feed her or untie her until night. Then the squaw cut her bonds and put a long rawhide thong around her neck. She was kicked to her feet and out of the tepee. She was led to water like a dog, and forced to drink on her hands and knees.

Then she was taken back, given a rawhide plate with a little cooked meat in the middle of it, and after she had eaten it, tied again.

She had not seen the Indian who had captured her all day. She waited, in a dull lethargy of fear, for his return.

But he did not come back. He had gone off again with a hunting and scouting party. And she fell into an exhausted, numbing sleep, from which she did not awake until she heard the volley of shots out beyond the village edge.

CHAPTER NINETEEN

As Luke had expected, it took the Indians a little time to recover from their surprise. He could imagine the scramble that was going on back in the village but for several minutes he had no time for anything but wildly desperate riding.

The Maxfields were close behind, and for the first time in his experience with them, they let eagerness rule in place of common sense. Still blissfully unaware of the Comanche village less than a quarter mile away, they emptied their guns at him like boys firing at jack-rabbits. It was only afterwards that he heard Gabe's voice roar, "Hold it! Look at all them goddam tracks! That son-of-a-bitch has . . ."

Luke thundered up out of a short draw on to a plateau. Looking behind, he could see the Comanche horse herd on a flat half a mile beyond the village. He could see mounted warriors pounding out away from it and was reminded of a hornet's nest when you stir it with a stick.

Again Gabe's roar, "That bastard's led us smack into the middle of a bunch of Injuns! Load up quick and let's get out of here!"

Luke swung his horse and galloped back down the draw. It wouldn't do to run off yet. Flight would only draw Comanches after him. The thing to do, for now, was to put the Maxfields between himself and the approaching warriors and keep them there if possible. At least until the fight was under way.

Accordingly, he left the draw before he reached the place where the Maxfields were and climbed its precipitous sides with his horse scrambling wildly for footing.

He was beginning to realize how foolish he had been to think he could pull this off. There were too many unforeseen difficulties. There were too many Indians. They'd surround not only the Maxfields but him as well.

Luke swung off his horse in a small thicket of mesquite and stood by the animal's head, holding the headstall. The Maxfields were bickering and quarrelling among themselves, but he knew their hands were busy loading their empty guns. How long should he stay here? How long? He had to get out before the Indians got behind him, but he didn't dare get out before most of them had left the village.

Even so, there wasn't much chance that he could successfully enter the village and get away with Nancy. There would be old men and boys in the village even after the warriors left. And some of the squaws could fight like men. Even if all the warriors were occupied with the Maxfields, Luke would still have the whole village to contend with.

But defeatism wasn't one of his failings. So he stood silently and waited until he heard the pound of the warriors' horses coming on.

He mounted now and, as silently as he could, threaded his way back up the draw. Instead of riding out on top of the plateau as he had before, he circled its foot, north, staying in the high brush that grew below its shallow rim.

Renewed firing broke out below. As quickly as it did, a howl went up from the gathering savages. Moccasined heels dug into their horses' sides. Galloping, they converged upon the sounds of firing coming from down below.

Luke didn't change his pace. He stayed at the foot of the bluff until he was well upstream. Then and only then did he drop down the brushy slope into the stream-bed and head towards the Indian camp.

Firing was general now back there where the Maxfields were. They, at least, were immobilized, probably permanently. He didn't see how any of them could escape, surrounded as they were by more than a hundred savages.

He hoped they fought long and well. He hoped they fought fiercely enough to keep the Indians occupied for several hours at least.

Several hundred yards from the village, Luke tied his horse. He hated to do it because he would be virtually helpless afoot. But he figured his best chance lay in stealth. There would be some guards in the village and to enter it on horseback would only draw them all to him, while he might be able to handle one or two if he encountered them singly.

Creeping along silently but quickly, he reached the edge of the high brush and could look into the village. Squaws, old men and children had gathered at the edge of the stream and were trying to see the fight, which was hidden from them by the rise of ground on the other side of the stream.

Low brush stretched away uphill along the edge of the camp. Luke flopped and began to work his way through it, a part of his mind concentrating on the sounds of the battle going on, another part listening for sounds approaching him.

After he had gone about twenty-five yards, he cautiously raised his head. Some of the squaws were wading across the stream and climbing the shallow hill beyond. Others kept the children back, or tried, but curiosity was too strong. Slowly, steadily, almost like a tide, the curious line of spectators moved across the stream and up the slope beyond.

Luke felt a surge of hope. If enough of them left the village and went to watch that fight, he might get in unseen.

He dropped his head and wormed his way forward, towards a lone tepee at the village edge. He raised his head again . . .

He saw the horse's hoofs not a dozen yards from where he lay, saw them first from a corner of his eye. Instantly his head swung and his glance raised. And he saw a Comanche brave riding towards him at the same instant the brave saw him.

Surprise touched the Comanche's eyes — surprise that lasted only the briefest instant. Then the man leaped from his horse and charged towards the spot Luke lay, drawing his knife as he did.

The brave was young — probably less than twenty or he would not have been assigned the duty of guarding the camp instead of being allowed to join the fight. His youth and reckless ambition led him to attack Luke by himself, rather than shouting out for help. He wanted to distinguish himself — Luke could see that in his eager, triumphant eyes.

Luke tried to rise, but there was no time. Before he could more than come to his hands and knees and start to rise, the brave was on him.

Luke raised the rifle, held in both hands, to break the force of the Indian's charge. The knife rang against the rifle steel and slipped down the barrel to inflict a deep gash in Luke's left hand.

Raising the rifle as he drove his body forward and up, Luke managed to pitch the Indian bodily over his head and afterwards he whirled like a cat, the rifle still held in both his hands.

Driving forward towards the Indian, who was still rolling, Luke brought the rifle down.

He slipped as he dived, and the rifle came down across the Indian's chest. A grunt escaped the young man's lips and immediately Luke dropped the rifle and clutched for the right wrist of the Indian, for the hand that held the knife.

His own left hand was slippery with blood, which gushed over the Indian's wrist. But he got it in both hands and wrenched with all his strength.

His hands slipped off. It was like trying to hold a trout flopping free on the grassy bank of a mountain stream.

Luke drove an elbow down on to the Indian's throat and heard him choke. He grasped for the knife hand again, catching it just before the knife plunged into his side.

This time his hands held on. The man's wrist had rubbed in the dust and was coated thickly with it.

He twisted viciously, and a sharp cry escaped the Indian's lips. The knife fell from his hand.

Luke grabbed for it and felt his hand close on its handle. Holding it, he clawed around, aware that now the Indian was trying to get away.

With his free left hand, he seized the Indian's breech-clout and tried to hold him. The Indian rolled, saw Luke's face and the knife in his hand.

He kicked out furiously, still trying to get away. In his eyes was the sudden fear of youth, the knowledge that ambition had led him too far along the road to destruction. He opened his mouth to yell . . .

Luke plunged the knife into his chest, throwing a forearm down across the Indian's throat as he did to stifle his cry. And lay there across the dying Indian's body until his struggles ceased.

Then, and only then, did he raise his head and look around. The commotion of the fight must have drawn attention; others would be coming . . .

But the village seemed deserted. Even the dogs seemed to have joined those slowly moving up the slope beyond the stream.

Luke got up and sprinted for the shelter of the nearest lodge. His heart was pounding in his chest, both from exertion and nervousness. The odds had improved but they were still too long. Someone must have remained behind. And it only took one cry of alarm.

He stopped behind the lodge. With the knife he slit its back and stepped inside.

It was deserted. He crossed it quickly and peered from the flap. There were nearly a hundred lodges in this village. How was he to know which held Nancy Holcomb prisoner?

There was no sure way to know. But there was one chance. Someone must be guarding her and probably wouldn't leave, particularly if the village was under attack.

He looked down the village street, but a little ways beyond him it curved, and he could see only as far as the curve. He stepped outside. A puppy that had stayed behind ran up to him, smelled his leg and backed away, hackles raised. The pup began to bark shrilly.

Luke threw a rock at him as he crossed the village street and ducked behind another tepee. The pup fled, yipping. Peering out from behind this one, Luke saw a single squaw standing before one of the lodges craning her neck towards the hill across the stream, trying to see.

Luke backed away. He retreated until he could cross to the row of tepees that contained the one she was guarding without being seen. Then he made his way watchfully, stealthily, back towards the spot.

He heard her muttering angrily and unintelligibly to herself. He slit the tepee back with infinite care and in almost complete silence. Peering inside, he saw Nancy Holcomb, tied hand and foot with her back towards him.

He pulled apart the slit he had made with a hand on each side and stepped in. Nancy started to roll, and he lunged for her and flung himself down across her body. His big hand clamped over her mouth.

For an instant, her eyes were wide, stricken with terror and surprise. Then they calmed, and Luke lifted his hand away from her mouth.

He cut the rawhide thongs on her hands and then on her feet, his back to the entrance flap. He saw her eyes widen and tried to turn . . .

Something heavy and very solid struck him a glancing blow on the side of the head. He pitched forward, falling across Nancy Holcomb's legs.

He was not quite unconscious, but he was near to it. Nancy rolled, unable to pull her legs from under him quickly enough, and wrapped her arms precariously around the squaw's legs. The squaw came down, trying to swing the stone tomahawk again but unable to do so because her right arm was pinned beneath her body.

Before she could roll, Nancy had freed her legs and reached her. They grappled fiercely, as savage as animals.

Groggy, Luke stood up. It would have been easy to kill the squaw, but he couldn't bring himself to do it. He knew something had to be done, however, and quickly too. Before the squaw began to screech.

No time for softness — he knew what this same squaw would do to him if he failed and was captured. He swung a foot, heel tipped, as her head came up, and caught her squarely on the ear.

She collapsed atop Nancy without a sound. Luke knelt and rolled her off. He was still groggy from the blow of the toma-hawk, and could feel his arm bleeding again.

Nancy whispered breathlessly, "I'm so glad . . . what are we going to do?"

"Get out of here. Just hope we aren't seen."

"Where are the others?" She tried her legs gingerly. They were wobbly from bad circu-lation, but she could walk.

"What others?"

"I thought . . . all that shooting . . ."

He studied her face briefly. She'd had a bad time and it showed, both in her appear-ance and in the expression her eyes held. But she wasn't beat — he could see that too. He said softly, "I'm all alone. That com-motion out there is the Maxfields. I led them here. Now let's get going before those bucks come back."

He poked his head out the slit at the rear of the tepee. He saw nothing but the pup, far down the street nosing a pile of hides.

He gripped her arm. "You've got nothing

to lose. We'll probably make it, but don't lose your head if things look bad."

She nodded, her eyes steadily on his face.

He stepped outside, and whispered, "Stay right behind me and do exactly what I do."

He slipped carefully away and Nancy stayed close behind. He still didn't believe this. It was too damned good to be true. Broad daylight — and he'd stolen a prisoner from a Comanche village.

Maybe they wouldn't find out until he was well away. Provided that squaw didn't come to and begin to yell. Provided none of those across the stream turned their heads and looked back. Provided they didn't run into a village guard.

He closed his mind to thoughts of failure and headed for the concealment of that low brush at the upper edge of the Indian camp.

CHAPTER TWENTY

They reached the edge of the village without incident, but Luke did not crowd his luck. Immediately he flopped to the ground and began to worm his way through the brush. Behind him, Nancy followed suit.

It seemed forever this time before he reached the cover of high brush and could rise to his feet. Glancing back, he saw that some of the people were walking back towards the village. Others were still standing just beneath the crest of the hill, watching the progress of the fight. There was not much firing any more, and from that fact Luke surmised that the Maxfields were almost finished.

A matter of time — and not much time at that — before someone discovered that Nancy was gone, before the unconscious squaw was found. When she was they'd pull forty or fifty braves away from the fight in the draw and put them to scouting for trail.

The dead brave would be found, and the trails he and Nancy had made.

Luke figured he had less than a half hour lead. Even if he wasn't seen. No time to catch another horse for Nancy from the Indians' herd. That was too risky anyway. She'd have to ride double with him.

They reached his horse and he boosted her up behind the saddle. He mounted, reined around and headed away from the camp. He circled it and beat his way south, crowding the horse to the animal's limit as soon as he thought he was clear.

Nancy's arms were around his waist. He could feel them trembling, with relief, with renewed hope, he supposed. He knew he should tell her that it was far too soon to hope. His horse was worn out from a night of hard riding and the Indians' horses were fresh. In addition, Luke's horse was carrying double weight.

Ten miles, fifteen. It was the most he could expect. But at least he was free for now, and Nancy was free, and the Maxfields were no longer a threat.

He kept looking behind nervously as he travelled, and did not try to ration the horse's remaining strength. Once, far to his left, he thought he saw a dust cloud raise. He watched the spot intently for several minutes, but did not see it again, and finally decided it had been stirred up by a twisting current of wind.

And riding, he marvelled at the courage of the girl riding behind him. She looked like bloody hell, he thought grinning, with her hair uncombed and dirty, with her clothes in rags, with her face and arms and legs dirty as a little boy's. But they hadn't broken her — neither the Maxfields nor the Indians. He looked around at her and she made an uncertain smile. "You were right."

"About what?"

"The Maxfields."

He grinned approvingly at her, but he didn't speak.

His horse was tiring faster, but he didn't dare let up. He kept glancing behind for signs of pursuit, and each time he did, he glimpsed her face. She was watching him steadily, her eyes calm, filled with faith and confidence. He had done the impossible, in her estimation at least, and she had faith that he could continue to do so. But he couldn't. It was one thing to slip into an Indian village when it was deserted and they didn't even know you were around, quite another to fight off fifty savages in an open battle.

He had gone no more than a dozen miles when he saw it coming on behind — a cloud of dust that raised twenty or thirty feet into the air.

He glanced ahead immediately, hoping she had not read his expression. Apparently she had not, for she didn't glance behind.

After that, he looked back only occasionally, and no oftener than he had before. Let her relax, if she could, in the belief that she was safe. Let her feel safe at least as long as possible.

The sun was directly overhead. He hadn't given much thought to the time and was a bit startled to realize the whole morning was gone. If he only had a little more lead than he had, another ten miles, he might have made it through until dark. But no use hoping for things that couldn't be.

And then he noticed something that puzzled him. The dust cloud raised by the pursuing Indians seemed to be drawing slightly to the left.

Steadily they drew that way. Luke rode through a notch in a bluff, and afterwards watched the notch intently from beyond. He hardly dared to hope, but he couldn't help the excitement that kept rising in his mind. That dust he had seen earlier on his left — could it be that one of the Maxfields had escaped? Could it be that the party of Indians had happened upon his trail instead of upon that of Luke and Nancy?

A mile beyond the notch, he stopped his horse, rode him down into a small depression and swung to the ground. If this wild new guess was right there was no use risking dust that the Indians might spot by chance.

Hardly daring to breathe, he watched that distant notch. And then he saw the Indians go thundering around the end of the bluff, avoiding the notch altogether.

Grinning, he looked at Nancy. "They're chasing someone else. They've got a different trail than ours."

Relief was so strong in him he felt like shouting. He unsaddled his horse and rubbed the animal down briskly with the saddle blanket. He picketed the horse to graze.

Nancy was strangely silent, but her eyes seldom left his face. He knew she was thinking ahead, to the time when he would leave her.

He didn't permit himself to think that far ahead. It was possible, even probable, that she no longer had a house. It had been left unguarded for several days. And even if it was still standing, the Maxfields who had escaped would lead the Comanches straight to it.

He let the horse rest for two hours. Then he saddled again, lifted Nancy up, and went on at a much more leisurely pace.

There was no longer a need for her arms around his waist but she kept them there and as they rode a strange wordless closeness grew between them.

No longer was there dust on the horizon. The Indians had passed to the left and on ahead. But he kept close watch anyway, determined not to be caught by surprise.

The sun dropped low in the west, and its colour changed from gold to orange, A cool breeze blew from out of the north.

The horse plodded on, his head down. And Nancy and Luke talked. She told him about her father, and Ben, and about her mother who was dead. She told him about her childhood, here in this place, and about Indian attacks that had, always before, been beaten off.

Her voice was pleasant and soft. The light faded in the sky and dusk came softly over the harsh, hot land. They were no more than half a dozen miles from the house when Luke thought he heard shots. A regular fusilade, like twenty or thirty men firing all at once.

After that, he heard sporadic shooting that seemed to be coming closer.

He shook his head imperceptibly. A vagary of the wind. Whichever one of the Maxfields it was that had escaped was under seige ahead there at the house. It only sounded like the shots were coming close.

But after another mile of riding, he knew he had been right. Fewer shots now, but they were definitely closer. Closer than the Holcomb house.

He frowned, puzzled. Maybe a posse had come out from Comanche Wells. It *had* to be white men chasing that bunch of Indian braves. It could be nothing else. Perhaps the Holcomb crew . . . perhaps they had re-turned.

He rode more cautiously and saw them at last in the fading light, fleeing along a ridge outlined against the darkening sky. He turned that way. To put fifty Indians to flight you had to have a considerable force. At least twenty or thirty men.

The shooting had stopped, and all was still. Luke came up the ridge on which he had seen the Indians and stared down at the sight he had never hoped to see again. A ranger camp.

They had apparently abandoned the pur-suit of the Indians for the night. Fires winked, small hot fires built from buffalo chips.

Nancy was trembling violently behind him. Luke said, "A ranger camp. Looks like we made it after all."

He felt weak with relief himself. He touched his horse's sides with the spurs and the animal plodded along down the slope.

They were challenged a hundred yards from the camp by a sentry, and afterwards rode on in. Luke slid off and lifted Nancy down.

The rangers wore no uniforms; they were dressed much the same as Luke was. He might have been one of them, too, for he possessed the same quiet, competent manner they did.

Their commander listened to Luke's and Nancy's stories with only an occasional question while they ate ravenously. "Then you reckon it was one of the Maxfields they was trailin' south? Any chance it was the one that killed the sheriff in Comanche Wells?"

Luke said, "I don't know which one of the Maxfields did that."

"I'll give you an escort back to the ranchhouse. I can spare a man or two. This bunch of bucks has been raisin' bloody hell. They've been burnin' an' scalpin' damn near as far south as Comanche Wells. Might be a few stragglers around."

Luke shook his head. "You only saw half the warriors in that village. You'll need every man you've got. We'll manage."

He gave the ranger a detailed description of the location of the village. They wanted him and Nancy to stay the night, but Luke shook his head. The house was standing yet, or had been when the rangers left it. With one of the Maxfields loose, anything could happen in the course of a night. He wanted to make sure it didn't.

So they mounted up and went on, fresh horses having been supplied by the commander of the rangers.

The distance was short between the camp and the house and they covered it in a little more than an hour, without talking much, a strange kind of tension between them.

Luke didn't tell Nancy, but he knew the trouble wasn't over yet. One of the Maxfields was alive, he was loose and as dangerous as a rabid wolf. His whole family had been wiped out, and he would blame just one man for that — Luke himself.

One thing only would be in his mind — vengeance, the destruction of the man responsible for the destruction of the Maxfield clan.

Luke had no way of knowing which one it was, but he had a peculiar feeling that the man was Gabe.

The house was dark, blending with the hill into which it was partly sunken. Luke drew rein three hundred yards away, and Nancy followed suit.

She seemed to know what was in his mind, for she asked no questions. He said, "Stay here," in a voice barely audible fifteen feet away.

"Be careful, Luke. Be careful."

He swung off his horse, pulling the rifle from the boot. He did not approach the house directly, but quartered away. He wanted nothing that would lead that lone, surviving Maxfield to Nancy, for with her as a hostage . . .

He approached from the west, taking each step carefully and as silently as he could. Nothing about the scene before him told him that someone was here. No horses were in the corral, none were visible in the yard. There was no light and there was no sound.

Luke didn't need these things. Something crawling along the upper part of his spine told him someone was here. His heart beat fast and his breathing was shallow and quick.

A premonition began to bother Luke, the

strangest thing he had ever felt. He had challenged the Maxfield clan successfully. He had invaded the Indian village and come away unscathed. He had faced certain death a dozen times in the last few days. But now . . .

Only Gabe possessed the toughness, the ruthlessness, the sharpness to have escaped the trap Luke had drawn him and his brothers into. It could only be Gabe down there, burning with hate, waiting like a silent, deadly wolf for just one thing — to kill Luke. And this time he might succeed.

Luke would need every bit of cunning he possessed to outwit Gabe. He would need more strength, more quickness than was left in him. None of the customary ruses would work.

He inched forward. His boot touched a rock and gave off a faintly scraping noise.

Nothing happened. The yard was silent, completely so. You'd think it was deserted, he thought. That was exactly what he was supposed to think.

Luke would have preferred an open fight, with light enough to see, and would have taken his chances willingly. But it was not his choice. He'd have to play this out Gabe Maxfield's way.

Again he moved forward, taking each step

with care. His ears strained for sound, his eyes strained into the darkness. His body was tense. His eyes ached and began to see things that weren't there.

Carefully, silently, he paced on, his knuckles white against the dark stock of the rifle.

A mouse rustled the grass, a dozen feet to his left and he whirled, raising the rifle, tightening his finger on the trigger.

He cursed himself silently. Quick movements like that made sound, sound that could kill him tonight.

The house made a dark, looming shape against the lighter darkness of the plain and the shallow hill immediately behind it. The air was cool, but Luke's body was soaked with sweat.

He still had no concrete evidence that Maxfield was here. He had heard nothing, seen nothing. He hoped anxiously that Nancy would remain exactly where she was and keep completely still.

He began to worry about her. What better way for Gabe to gain an advantage than to find Nancy? The sounds she and Luke had made arriving might have been heard by a silent, listening man at the house.

He frowned angrily. Gabe's nerves were surely as tight as his own, as near the breaking point.

An idea began to burn in his mind. A mouse had made him whirl. A sound might make Gabe move quickly too.

Luke stopped. Kneeling, he laid his rifle carefully on the ground. He removed his boots, one at a time, with infinite care.

He laid one boot on the ground about two feet to his right. Holding the other in his right hand, he picked up his rifle with his left. He eased silently to his feet.

A boot crashing against the side of the house — it wouldn't fool Gabe, but it might startle him before he had a chance to think.

Luke drew back his hand. He threw the boot, hard, towards the house.

It whirred faintly as it passed through the air and then slammed against the solid side of the house with what seemed like a thunderous crash.

Luke wasn't listening for the crash of the boot; he wasn't even facing that way. He was turned, trying to exclude the sound of the boot from his ears, listening for another, softer sound.

And he heard it, though he couldn't definitely place its location — a sibilant sound of something scraping against clothing.

Gabe's rifle, he supposed, raised in an instinctive, startled gesture. Now he knew,

knew for sure that Gabe was here. And he knew Gabe was beyond him, away from the house.

Luke stopped breathing altogether and waited. The sound he heard was softer than the other had been. But it was a sound, and he placed the exact location of it.

He eased the air out of his lungs and drew another cautious breath even as he began to move. He headed for the sound, straining his eyes into the darkness even more intently than he had before.

This was beginning to tell on him, after the tension and anxiety of the long day past. He wanted to shoot blindly into the darkness, to draw Gabe's fire even if Gabe's bullets found him. He wanted to shout, to force Gabe into the open.

He gripped the rifle even tighter instead. This would be more difficult than anything that had gone before. Again the odd little premonition touched his mind.

But his movement didn't stop. And he made no sound.

At a dozen yards Gabe's form would show up against the lighter shade of the plain. He must close the distance between them to a dozen yards, and he had to see Gabe first.

He was certain now that it was Gabe he faced. None of the others would have been this shrewd.

A light breeze stirred, blowing from Luke's left. As it did, his eyes glittered suddenly in the darkness. That breeze might save his life.

There was one thing Gabe wouldn't think of. His smell. Gabe was counting on sight and hearing. His nose was so used to his own rank smell that he was probably no longer aware of it. But if Luke could get downwind he could follow Gabe's smell directly to the man just as an animal does.

Immediately, Luke quartered away from the course he was following by turning right and putting the wind at his back. He travelled with the utmost care for more than fifty feet. Then he turned again, praying silently that the breeze wouldn't die too soon.

Like a shadow he moved, his eyes and ears alert, his nostrils flared as he keened the breeze.

A rank, wild smell it was when it came along the wind. A smell of rancid grease, of sweat and tobacco, of campfire smoke and lather flecked off a running horse's neck.

And strong — so strong it made the flesh crawl along Luke's neck. He stood frozen, and the smell began to fade.

Gabe was moving, as he was, stalking through the darkness. Luke turned and backtracked and the smell grew strong again.

He swung into the wind. Now every nerve, every muscle was tight as a Comanche bowstring. Quartering into the wind, he followed Gabe's smell, searching the darkness ahead.

No shot had been fired, no hostile move made by either man. But the hostility, the hatred, the will to kill was there in the air, as tangible as smoke or fog, as deadly as the venom of a rattlesnake.

A shadow ahead, fleeting and vague. Instantly Luke snapped his rifle up and fired.

Flame shot from the muzzle of the gun, blinding him momentarily. Black powder-smoke that appeared greyish white in darkness made a cloud between him and the shadowy form of Gabe Maxfield ahead, obscuring his view and making a second shot momentarily impossible.

He flung himself aside, scrambling, even as the flame of the muzzle flare died away. He ran a full twenty feet before he stopped and whirled again.

Sounds back there — the harsh sounds of a man breathing, a man in pain. But regular breathing, which meant to Luke that Gabe was neither dying nor even seriously hurt.

And now he faced a Gabe more danger-ous than before, if that were possible. He faced a wounded animal at bay, who had no fear of death except that death might cheat him of his prey.

Gabe's voice — a — whisper — came out of the blackness of the night. "Go ahead, you son-of-a-bitch! Shoot again. Shoot at the sound of my voice."

Luke didn't answer. But he moved. He put himself between Gabe and the place he had left Nancy Holcomb on the hill. He knew now that Gabe would find her if he could.

And then, suddenly, the thing Luke had been dreading happened. That shot and the ensuing silence had frightened her. Gabe's whisper had been too low for her to hear.

She called, "Luke! Luke! Are you all right?"

Behind him and off to the left she was. Gabe's breathing was silent again.

Luke retreated. He couldn't take the chance that Gabe would circle and pass him undetected.

He backed carefully forty or fifty feet. Then he turned and ran, away from the house, up the hill towards the place where Nancy was. He was drawing danger to her, but if Gabe reached her first, Gabe had won the fight.

The dark shapes of the horses loomed ahead against the sky. And another shape came running out from them.

Luke struck her with his diving body just below the knees. He heard her sharp cry of terror and surprise, but had no thought of it now. For behind, lancing wickedly out of the night, Gabe's rifle cracked again and again.

Bullets tore through the air over Luke's and Nancy's heads. One of them struck Luke's horse and the animal went thrashing to his knees, effectively overriding the sounds that Gabe was making as he came.

Luke felt the violent trembling of Nancy's body against his own. From the ground he saw the rapidly looming shape of Gabe, limping, shambling along like a gigantic, maddened bear.

He couldn't shoot — that would draw Gabe's fire and put Nancy in mortal danger.

He lunged away from her, rising as he went. He headed straight for Gabe. The man might kill him, but the time for stealth was past. Gabe was charging directly at them, and would have blundered on them anyway.

Fifteen feet. Luke's finger was tight on the trigger of his rifle. He was ready to fire, but suddenly he had no target. Smart and shrewd and tough as a badger to the end, Gabe had worked his last deadly ruse. He had flung himself to the ground, eliminating himself as a target for Luke but giving himself a chance for a clear, killing shot.

And the shot came, blasting wickedly out of the darkness close to the ground ahead.

It tore into Luke at the side of his neck, searing like a branding iron, drawing an instant rush of blood that ran down his neck and drenched his shirt below.

His rifle muzzle swung downward; his finger pulled against the trigger. The rifle leaped with recoil in his hands.

Straight at the flash he fired, and heard the bullet clang against the steel barrel of Gabe's gun and go whining away into the night.

Then he was over Gabe, on him. Gabe's rifle roared again, almost in his face. The bullet tore through the muscles of his upper arm, numbing the arm instantly, almost making him drop his gun.

He swung it like a club, and heard the steel barrel thud against Gabe's shaggy head. He heard, too, the ring of steel against steel as his gunbarrel struck that of Gabe and flung it aside.

He tripped on Gabe's wildly thrashing

body and plunged beyond, falling.

Rolling frantically, he faced around and came to his knees. Gabe's rifle roared again, almost in his face.

He fired at the flash, and at the bulk of the man himself behind it, fired instantly and without conscious thought.

A monstrous grunt drove out of Gabe. His empty rifle came flying through the air towards Luke to strike him squarely in the chest.

And all was still before him. All was still where Gabe was but not beyond, where the dying horse still thrashed violently, where Nancy Holcomb breathed noisily, shallowly with terror.

Holding his rifle ready, Luke got up. He couldn't remember how many times he had fired and didn't know whether the rifle was empty or not.

He reached Gabe's sprawled-out form. He stirred it with his foot.

Wholly limp it was, without life or movement of breathing. Gabe Maxfield was dead at last.

He stepped over Gabe and called, "Nancy? It's all right. It's all right now."

He heard her coming, running, and there could be no more tension and strain between them — not ever again. She fled to his arms with a force that knocked the breath from him and her tears were soft and warm and wet against his stubbled cheek. He lowered his head and kissed her, firmly and possessively, on the mouth. Luke Partin was home, and Nancy was home too, in his arms.

ABOUT THE AUTHOR

Lewis B. Patten wrote more than ninety Western novels in thirty years and three of them won Spur Awards from the Western Writers of America and the author himself the Golden Saddleman Award. Indeed, this highlights the most remarkable aspect of his work: not that there is so much of it, but that so much of it is so fine. Patten was born in Denver, Colorado, and served in the U.S. Navy 1933–1937. He was educated at the University of Denver during the war years and became an auditor for the Colorado Department of Revenue during the 1940s. It was in this period that he began contributing significantly to Western pulp magazines, fiction that was from the beginning fresh and unique and revealed Patten's lifelong concern with the sociological and psychological effects of group psychology on the frontier. He became a professional writer at the time of his first novel, *Mas-*

sacre at White River (1952). The dominant theme in much of his fiction is the notion of justice, and its opposite, injustice. In his first novel it has to do with exploitation of the Ute Indians, but as he matured as a writer he explored this theme with significant and poignant detail in small towns throughout the early West. Crimes, such as rape or lynching, were often at the centre of his stories. When the values embodied in these small towns are examined closely, they are found to be wanting. Conformity is always easier than taking a stand. Yet, in Patten's view of the American West, there is usually a man or a woman who refuses to conform. Among his finest titles, always a difficult choice, surely are *A Killing at Kiowa* (1972), *Ride a Crooked Trail* (1976), and his many fine contributions to Doubleday's Double D series, including *Villa's Rifles* (1977), *The Law at Cottonwood* (1978), and *Death Rides a Black Horse* (1978). His later books include *Tincup in the Storm Country* (1996), *Trail to Vicksburg* (1997), *Death Rides the Denver Stage* (1999), and *The Woman at Ox-Yoke* (2000).

We hope you have enjoyed this Large Print book. Other Thorndike, Wheeler, Kennebec, and Chivers Press Large Print books are available at your library or directly from the publishers.

For information about current and upcoming titles, please call or write, without obligation, to:

Publisher
Thorndike Press
295 Kennedy Memorial Drive
Waterville, ME 04901
Tel. (800) 223-1244

or visit our Web site at:

http://gale.cengage.com/thorndike

OR

Chivers Large Print
published by BBC Audiobooks Ltd
St James House, The Square
Lower Bristol Road
Bath BA2 3SB
England
Tel. +44(0) 800 136919
email: bbcaudiobooks@bbc.co.uk
www.bbcaudiobooks.co.uk

All our Large Print titles are designed for easy reading, and all our books are made to last.

APL		CCS	
Cen		Ear	
Mob		Cou	
ALL		Jub	
WH		CHE	
Ald		Bel	
Fin		Fol	
Can		STO	
Til		HCL